RICHARD M PEARSON

A GHOST IN THE GLEN

This is a work of fiction. Names, characters, places, and incidents either are the product of the author's imagination or are used fictitiously. Any resemblance to actual persons, living or dead, events, or locales is entirely coincidental.

Copyright © Richard M Pearson 2022

All rights reserved. No part of this book may be reproduced or used in any manner without written permission of the copyright owner except for the use of quotations in a book review.

First Edition

Cover Design by Ryan Tobias Thomas

All rights reserved

A Ghost in the Glen is the seventh book by Richard M Pearson.

This journey started with the release of my first novel, *The Path* in 2018. It was initially planned to be a one-off, but life has a habit of taking you down a different road than the one you expect. There is a saying that everybody has one book to write and that was supposed to be mine. After some lovely feedback and positive reviews, I decided to do a follow-up called, *Deadwater*. From that point on I seemed to get a small but loyal cult following who encouraged me to keep writing. Each time I finish a new book, I feel it may be my last, who knows? All I can say is that writing has proven to be a journey with many twists and turns, just like my books I suppose. In fact, just like life.

I was born in England and then lived in Wales and Northern Ireland before finally landing in Bonnie Scotland at the impressionable age of eight. You could call me multi-cultural but in a homely sort of way. My stories tend to be based in Scotland, a country I have a deep passion for. Having said that, travel does make the heart grow fonder so I will occasionally take you to other dark and distant lands.

Reading has always been one of my great passions. I love books that build up a gothic atmosphere of foreboding, the first half of *Dracula* by Bram Stoker being a classic example. In my opinion, a good book should always have an unexpected finale. I will never forget reading *Rebecca* by Daphne Du Maurier and the way the twist turned the whole story on its head.

I hope that by the time you have finished this book you will have enjoyed the journey into the dark corners of your imagination. As I mentioned before, we all have the potential to write a book. Maybe mine will inspire you to give it a go as well.

The Border country of Scotland will always be my spiritual home. It has been many years since I lived there but my heart always seems to be drawn back to that land of vast forested hills, hidden towns, and quiet winding little roads. It was a weeklong walk from Portpatrick to Sanquhar through lonely Galloway in 2012 that inspired me to write my first ghost story, *The Path*. Since then I have revisited the area many times in my follow-up novels.

For this book, I have ventured further North in some of the stories. The Highlands of Scotland are both beautiful and spectacular. These days they no longer seem as remote as they were in my youth. Now the much-improved roads and better weather bring the tourists flocking to the Lochs and Glens. Maybe my stories yearn for a quieter time when life seemed simpler and you could sense the feeling of isolation as the long winters descended. The perfect setting then for these dark tales of drifting shadows and ghosts of the forgotten.

My previous books have been dedicated to the two most important people in my life, My wife Maureen and my daughter Lauren as well as my mother, father, and sisters. This time I want to mention those people we meet almost by accident and yet they become a major part of who we are. Those close friends who stick by us for better or for worse. You know who you are and there are too many to mention individually. Having said that I will dedicate this book to my two lifelong best friends. Paul Devlin who I first met in 1970 and shared many wild adventures with, and Syd my walking, cycling, and hill-climbing companion. She is one of those rare people who never judges me. These two amazing pals have helped to inspire many of the tales in this book.

Table of Contents

In Memory of Emily Mancini..........................12

First Love...36

Floodland...68

Jo-Jo...107

Money Can Buy Me, Love............................147

The Watcher 186

In Memory of the True Rab Gifford 234

A Ghost in the Glen

There is something about the tall mountains and lonely forests that make Scotland the perfect setting for these dark and macabre stories. Maybe it is the solitude you can find within minutes of leaving the city. Could it be the way the mist can quickly descend from the hills to leave you feeling alone and isolated? This is a country that remains trapped by the history of ancient past battles, a people still searching for their true identity in the world. A once proud Kingdom now ruled by others. This is Scotland, the land of ghosts.

This book contains seven dark tales set in the beautiful glens and countryside of my nation, Scotland. I dare you to seek out The Watcher who preys on those we love, escape to Ben Nevis as the floods close in, weep with the man who can never be free of his dead mother, and walk beside the boy who will always wonder if his first love was only a figment of his imagination.

Hopefully, these strange stories will help you survive the bleak winter evenings as the streets empty and the cold cruel rain swirls through the statuesque trees. I implore you to stay curled up safely in your bed reading, for outside they will surely be waiting for you. The moon has risen, and night is on your doorstep. Sleep well, my friend.

In Memory of Emily Mancini

'Bless me Father for I have sinned. It's a good few years since I last came to confession.'

'How many years are you talking about? A few, five, ten?' The priest spoke the words softly although they lacked any real emotion. On the opposite side of the confessional, Brendon stared into the gloom at the wooden slatted window that separated the two men. The stale smell that permeated the booth added to his feeling of being isolated, alone in the world with just his guilt to keep him company.

'Sorry Father. Yes, a long time. I don't think I've been to confession since I was a child, in fact, I haven't even been to church in the last 30 years. I am so sorry Father, is it ok for me to be here?' He could sense the priest sitting up and taking notice. Maybe he could already tell that this one might be slightly more interesting than the usual ten-year-old asking for forgiveness for being cheeky or some old lady only there because faith's dull routine required her presence.

'There is no need to apologise, maybe after our chat today you will feel happier about returning to your faith to find comfort and salvation.' Brendon felt awkward kneeling to face a talking window. Already he was regretting starting this whole thing. Beads of sweat were trickling down his brow, small droplets of liquid guilt falling onto the sacred floor of God's sanctuary. He was not religious; he did not even believe in the Catholic faith anymore. But he knew he needed help, just someone to talk to, someone who would have no choice but to listen. Someone he would not need to look at while he told his story.

'So, what is it you would like to confess?' Father Mancini could sense the hesitancy on the other side of the booth. Long monotonous years of listening to the same old stories, the repeated small-scale crimes against Christianity, the pleading for eternal life, all of it had honed him to be instantly aware when something less mundane was coming his way. He edged forward in his seat, ready to be judge and juror, ready to be God.

'It's, it's nothing I have actually done Father, it's more to do with what is happening to me.' Brendon could feel his fingers gripping the small wooden shelf that sat under the slats of the opening. He could make out the shape of the priest's upper torso in the gloom on the other side of the booth. The voice in his head was talking to him again as the perspiration trickled down to the end of his nose and dripped onto the floor.

For heaven's sake Brendon. This is ridiculous, this man is going to think you're crazy. What on earth are you doing here? Just tell him something, anything and get the hell out of it.

Suddenly the booth vibrated as the confessor jumped abruptly to his feet. Father Mancini grabbed the handrail on his side to hold himself steady in his seat. He went to speak but he knew it was already too late. Brendon was pushing his way out through the curtain that covered the entrance to the little wooden chamber.

'My son, my son, wait. There is nothing that cannot be resolved by embracing the will of God Almighty. There is nothing you have done that cannot be forgiven in the eyes of the Lord Jesus Christ.' Brendon stopped in his tracks and turned to face the loud voice emanating from the curtain on the other side of the booth.

'It's not what I've done, Father. It is what is being done to me. Who in the Lord's name is he? Who in heaven's name is watching me?' With those last few words, Brendon was gone. The sound of his boots could be heard echoing around the walls of the cavernous old church as he ran to the exit and freedom.

Father Mancini sat back in his chair. This had been more excitement than he usually had in a whole year. He pondered the situation and then smiled. The priest did not expect to see the stranger come back again. It was a pity because whatever he was involved in, it had sounded rather interesting. *Maybe the man was crazy or on drugs, maybe he really was being followed. Oh well, I doubt it's worth worrying about.* The priest stood up and straightened his cassock before slowly leaving the booth. He desperately needed a cup of tea and one of Mrs. Taggart's shortbread biscuits. The old woman might have been off tune when she played the church organ, but she certainly knew how to make a nice bit of shortbread. He patted his large protruding stomach and walked with an air of superiority toward the side door that connected to his apartment.

'Bless me, Father, for I have sinned. It has been eight months since I last came to confession.'

On the other side of the booth, Father Mancini gave a quiet sigh and studied his fingernails before placing the middle digit of his left hand inside his mouth. He thought he vaguely recognised the voice talking to him from the other side of the panel. He had learned to cope with the boredom of endless confessions by zoning out, being there while not being there as he liked to call it.

'Would you like to confess your sins today?' He spoke the words while still chewing on his fingernail.

'It's not sinning I wish to confess today, Father.' Brendon spoke the words softly, trying to conceal the desperation he felt inside. Father Mancini suddenly sat up in his padded seat, recognition beginning to seep through the ancient wooden booth. He knew the voice now; it was that troubled man who had run out of the church last year.

'Well if you are not here today to confess, how else may I help you?' The priest was desperate to hear the man's story. Not because he cared for him, it was more to do with his own long-repressed feelings of guilt. The very reason he had moved into priesthood had been to hide his sins in the all-encompassing canopy of faith. Surely that was how it all worked? Guilt was built into the very fabric of the walls, it hung in the silent dusty air of the church and filled the lungs of the confessors, the altar boys, the organist, and yes, even Father Mancini.

Brendon leaned forward until his lips were almost touching the wooden slats. The priest imagined he could hear the man's pulsing heart beating in his chest.

'I am here because of him. He's back, Father. You sorted it out last time. I need you, beg you, to do the same again.' Mancini had stopped chewing on his nails now. His thoughts raced as he tried to take in what the man was saying. *This guy sounds off his head. Well, let's play along, see where this leads too. Anything is better than listening to old Jones moaning about lusting after the woman next door or Mrs. Taggart twittering on about the upcoming ladies coffee morning.*

'I don't follow you. What is it you think I did to help you the last time you came to confess?'

'Look, Father…' Brendon's voice was starting to rise in pitch. He coughed and tried to regain his composure. 'The thing, that thing that follows me. After I came here last time it stopped, it stopped stalking me, fucking watching me, but it's back, its back. It disappeared for six months after you fixed it, but it's back now, back even worse.' Brendon was becoming hysterical, his fingers again clutching the wooden sill tightly. Father Mancini interjected quickly to try and calm the confessor down in case he took flight again. He desperately wanted to know the rest of the story. For years he had waited for something big, something that might make him feel better about his own situation. Did the person with more guilt than the priest exist? Maybe, just maybe, this was the man.

'My son, my son, take a deep breath and try to calm down. I am here to help you, but you must calm down. Please can I also ask you not to use profanity in the house of the Sacred Lord?' Brendon sat back and tried to exhale the air that was trapped in his bursting lungs. He took out a tissue and mopped his brow before putting the wet paper back into his coat pocket.

'I'm sorry, Father.' The priest moved closer to the window and tried to keep his voice as soothing as possible.

'Now, why don't you start at the beginning and explain what it is that you think is going on? Without knowing the detail then it's difficult for me to be able to offer you the comfort that only the Lord Christ can give.'

* * *

Father Mancini lounged by the large fire in the spacious clergy house attached to the Church of the Sacred Heart. He did not look like a man of God as he lay stretched out with his feet perched on one of the chairs. His cassock was discarded on the floor exposing the casual attire that he kept hidden underneath. A pair of faded black shorts, a well-worn dark t-shirt and long black socks covered his sagging body. His right arm occasionally rose in a slow methodical motion to allow his fingers to dip the biscuit into his mug of tea. Pieces of damp digestive dotted his t-shirt and dripped down the side of his mouth. The priest had long ago discarded any formality when he was alone. What was the point? Other than his cleaner, Mrs. O'Connor, the only other visitors were usually officially booked appointments. He had no immediate family now that his mother was dead. She had been the one shining light in his life, the only person he had ever really loved. The one person he had ever really been allowed to love. Now in his early sixties, Father Mancini wearily accepted the fate he had been given many years previously. He had chosen to be alone because it allowed him to hide. The mask of the church let him keep his real emotions and sexuality hidden amongst the dust and the forgotten gravestones. Now all that remained was him and his fading guilt stuck in the same monotonous routine.

Until today of course. The priest thought back to the tale the strange confessor had told him and he smiled. *This was more like it, something different at long last. Someone who might even make him feel better about his own past.* With a little coaxing, the man had nervously tumbled out the words to his story. It all started a few years back when he was in his late twenties. He had a good job working as a train driver having been promoted to covering the main line railway between Glasgow in Scotland and Carlisle in England. The increased responsibility and difficult working hours had impacted his social life and although he enjoyed his job, it meant he had little time for friends and even less for a steady girlfriend. He would occasionally visit his parents in Dumfries but would make this coincide with his younger brother being away. He and Connor had never been close. They acted as though they hated the sight of each other. Being the only two siblings and with just two years between them, they had spent most of their childhood competing and fighting with each other over everything and nothing. Connor had always been the quiet one, the loner, while Brendon had grown up with a close circle of friends.

Over the years Brendon had come to accept that his brother suffered from depression. He tried to make allowances, but it had been difficult. He himself had found it hard to make his way through adolescence and his teenage years without a morose petulant younger brother to deal with as well. In the last few months before Brendon finally left home the two boys had come to serious blows. A lot of things had been said that both of them lived to regret. Since that day they had hardly spoken a word despite their parents trying to reconcile them. That was the problem for Brendon, his father expected him to be the peacemaker. Go cap in hand and beg for forgiveness from his brother when everyone knew that Connor was the problem in the relationship rather than him. The fact that he still lived with his parents in Dumfries and struggled to hold down a job proved the point. The endless bouts of alcoholism and recovery, all paid for by his parents surely helped to add proof to Brendon's argument.

As he told the priest the next part of the story the confessor had started to weep. The priest remembered hearing the drip of his tears as they fell to the floor of the booth. How much Brendon now wished he could go back and speak just one last time to his brother. Hold out the hand of friendship and forgiveness before it was too late. Father Mancini had wanted to say, *do you only now wish this because of your guilt rather than any affection for your brother?*

Tragedy had struck just over two years ago. It had always been coming, everyone sensed it. The inevitable conclusion to a life lived in torment. Connor had been found floating face down in a local loch not far from the family home. The verdict had been accidental death but most reckoned that he had committed suicide. He had tried many times before and some including Brendon had always dismissed each incident as yet another attention-seeking episode.

Of course, Brendon admitted to the priest that he felt guilt over the loss of his brother. Consoling his distraught parents and helping deal with the funeral arrangements had made it all a blur during the first weeks of Connor's death. Maybe he had even felt a sense of relief at times even though it was hard to admit it. Then as the months passed Brendon started to feel the guilt creep in. He was not sure if this was because he really felt that way or because he sensed that his parents blamed him in some way for what had happened. The words were never said but the moments of strained silence that would interrupt their conversation when his brother was mentioned would say it all.

The next piece of the tale was where things had become strange. It was this part that the priest had found most disturbing. Apparently just months after his brother's death Brendon had started seeing something, or at least thinking he saw something. Occasionally he would catch sight of a figure watching him, either standing outside his flat on dark evenings or brushing past him through the crowd as he walked to the front of his train at the busy Glasgow Central railway station. It had all come to a head when he started seeing the shape standing on isolated hills or at the side of the track as he pounded through the countryside at the controls of the massive machine. Before long he had to feign sickness from his work in case the hallucinations might make him miss a red signal and cause an accident. In desperation, he had visited Father Mancini the first time and the very next day the apparition was gone.

For the next six months, all seemed to go well, and Brendon had returned to his work. He had even been spending as much time as he could with his still-grieving parents. This was even though he could sense that his father still held him partly responsible for the loss of his brother. *Why did you have to hate him so much, why did there have to be so much rivalry between the two of you?*

Of course, the apparition eventually returned but this time it was worse. Father Mancini almost chuckled to himself as he recounted the rest of the crazy story. Not only did the vision re-appear but now it was truly haunting him. Brendon even said he could sense it sitting in the train cab beside him. He had tried to convince himself that it did not exist and then one day he had turned, and it was there, staring straight at him. In sheer panic, he had lost concentration and the express train had gone through two sets of red warning lights at speed before the automatic breaks had kicked in. He was immediately suspended pended medical reports. With little else to do Brendon had hidden inside his house but each evening there would be a faint knocking at the door. When he would answer there would be no one there. And then it appeared inside the house one morning, standing staring at him from the end of the hall. Brendon had fled and that was when he had arrived at the House of God yesterday. The only person in the world who could help him was Father Mancini. He had exorcised him once before, surely, he could do it again.

The priest did chuckle this time as he reached for another biscuit. He had of course told the stranger he needed to get medical help. He was seeing the apparition because he felt guilty about his brother. *My son, you need to seek professional counselling and with God's guidance, you will be rid of this feeling that your brother's death was caused directly by you.* The priest had started to grow impatient by the time the man concluded his story. Father Mancini had other appointments and tried to hurry Brendon along. The confessor was simply just relieved to have been granted an audience with the priest. He was convinced that the meeting would at least temporally end his misery.

The priest stretched his legs to allow his already warm toes to creep closer to the fire. His long fingers picked up yet another biscuit from the plate and dipped it into the tea that sat perched beside him on the arm of the chair. He winced as the cold liquid dripping from the end of the digestive touched his lips. The large clock on the mantelpiece above the fire ticked the endless seconds away as it marched relentlessly on towards eternity. Mancini was surprised to see he had been lying prostrate on the chair for more than an hour. The man's story had fascinated him. Not because he believed any of the nonsense about a ghost but because the guilt the confessor felt in some small way resonated with the way he felt, or at least had felt in the dim and distant past.

* * *

'Bless me, Father, for I have sinned. It has been 24 hours since I last came to confession.'

The priest was surprised and slightly irritated to see the man back so soon. He had expected him to disappear for six months and then return with another story about seeing things that simply did not exist. Father Mancini had enjoyed the excitement of the stranger's tale but not his quick return. Now he was worried that this might lead to the man appearing regularly and becoming a nuisance. He already had countless confessors who came week in, week out to repeat the same old boring tales of guilt. The last thing he needed was yet another one.

'How may I help you today? Have you forgiven yourself in the eyes of God and moved forward with your life?' Brendon was kneeling on the other side of the booth and felt like he wanted to scream with joy. The apparition was gone, exactly the same as had happened when he first came to visit The Church of the Sacred Heart.

'He, I mean it has gone. Even if it is just for a few months I can accept that. And, I have the comfort of knowing you will always be here to help me, Father.' The priest felt unsettled hearing that the man saw him as his saviour. *This madman needs professional help*. Mancini could not stop himself though, he wanted to know more.

'My son, as you know, the almighty God has guided you to redemption. But, can I ask you something further?' Brendon lifted his head and answered slowly, wondering what the priest was about to say.

'Yes, yes, of course, Father. What is it you desire to know?'

'Well, you have never mentioned what this apparition or thing you see resembles. You said *he* a moment ago. Can you elaborate further for me?' On the other side of the booth, Brendon could feel beads of sweat starting to run down his brow. A full twenty seconds passed before he spoke the words, so softly that the priest could hardly make them out. Yet, both of them already knew what the other was thinking.

'The apparition is my brother. My dead brother is haunting me.' The priest nodded to himself before replying.

'Is there any reason why your brother's spirit would be following you?' Again, Brendon did not answer at first. The words he wished to speak were stuck in his throat. He tried to get them out but all that his vocal cords could muster was a choking gargled sound. He stood up abruptly and steadied himself against the wooden panel of the booth. His head was swimming as fear enveloped him like a thick black cloud. He was already moving towards the curtain, towards freedom and away from the mist of guilt that was drowning his lungs. The priest heard the words amidst the panic of the confessor's quick escape. The booth shook to the sound of crashing boots as the answer floated across the stale air of the church.

'Oh God, yes. I know of many reasons why he could haunt me, but only one reason why he does haunt me.'

Mancini stood amongst the graves that surrounded the church of the Sacred Heart. A light wind was forcing itself through the headstones and bending the overgrown grass that bordered many of the forgotten monuments. The spring morning sun would occasionally break through the cloud only to disappear again, leaving him shivering in the gloom as he stared at the words carved in the granite.

> IN MEMORY OF A DEAR MOTHER
> EMILY MANCINI
> 6 AUGUST 1924
> 19 DECEMBER 1990
> SHOULD WE LOSE EACH OTHER IN THE
> SHADOW OF THE EVENING TREES

I WILL WAIT FOR YOU
AND SHOULD I FALL BEHIND
WAIT FOR ME

It had been a long time since he had felt the need to walk to this corner of the churchyard. In the first years after she had left him, he would religiously stand at the headstone each morning to confess his sins to his dead mother. It was the only way he could keep his guilt in check. *Confess to the Lord Almighty and everything would be forgiven.* It was with mixed emotions that he now stared at the words carved in the marble. They were already fading, and a green haze was starting to creep up from the bottom of the headstone. Just another lump of rock dedicated to someone who was drifting away into the ether. Once he was gone then she too would finally be forgotten.

Emily Mancini had controlled her son's life. He had never known anything different; he had never wanted it to be different. She had brought him up on her own from the day he had been born. A woman of the faith, a woman destined to live under the all-encompassing veil of the Catholic Church. Her husband Edoardo Mancini had died in the latter days of the second world war. She loved him with everything she had. The only man Emily had ever been with. The tragedy of him surviving through innumerable battles and horrors only to run out of luck just as the tide was turning had not been lost on her. The son who was growing inside her womb would be a shrine to Edoardo, a precious gift from God who would live in the eyes of The Lord.

Father Mancini could stand it no longer. The cold was biting into his bones and he could feel her words of anger and retribution floating out of the damp earth and into his soul. He was questioning why he was here. *Why walk to her gravestone after all these years? Why re-open the old wounds and forever torment yourself?* But of course, he knew the reason. He was back here because of the stranger. The man who thought his dead brother was haunting him. The priest understood what was happening quite clearly now. The similarity between the confessor and the priest's situation was the reason. He had tried over the years to block out that night when he had suffocated the emaciated woman who controlled his every move. Was it possible to love and hate someone so much that death was your only release?

Mancini knew the man would be back. He had to return so that he could learn the reason why the confessor was being haunted. Only then might the priest finally be able to lay his own personal ghosts to rest. He turned to walk back to the warmth of the church house and once more into the shroud of God that allowed him to live with his guilt. As he moved away, he turned back for one last look at the rotting gravestone and whispered the words that only he would ever hear. *Mother, maybe we will meet again one day, but I fear it will not be in heaven.*

* * *

'Bless me, Father, for I have sinned. It has been exactly eight days since I last came to confession.' The agitation and fear in the man's voice gave comfort to the priest. He knew he was in control now. This would maybe even be the last visit. The confessor was back and this time he would have to tell the whole story, or his tormentor would surely drive him over the edge.

'I take it the apparition has returned, my son. It seems it is back quicker this time, maybe sooner than you had expected?' Mancini spoke the words softly, he had the power, he held all the cards and Brendon had nothing to give in return.

'Yes, Father. I thought I would get more time, but it returned yesterday and now it's with me everywhere I go.'

'Even with you today, I mean are you saying the spirit is here now, in this very church?'

'Yes, yes Father. It's sitting outside in the seat opposite the one I was on before I came into the booth to confess.' The priest leaned forward; this was a new turn in the man's madness. He could hear Brendon whimpering on the other side of the confessional. Mancini had to find out why his victim believed he deserved to be haunted. *Ask the question before he runs away again, quickly ask him now.*

'Try to calm down. I promise that if you tell me everything then in the eyes of God you will finally be forgiven.' The words floated across to Brendon like a beacon of light. The priest was telling him that if he confessed then it would finally be over. The beads of sweat were still dripping from his brow but now the sound of them hitting the sacred floor gave him hope of salvation at last.

'Father, are you telling me that if I confess, I, I mean, tell you what really happened then the lord will forgive me and banish the ghost that torments me?' The priest shifted impatiently on the padded seat at the opposite side of the booth. Mancini wanted the man to confess, tell him what he had done so that the priest could finally be free of his own guilt.

'Yes, yes, tell me, confess your sins and in the eyes of God you will be forgiven.' An air of impatience was creeping into the priest's voice.

Brendon was weeping now, the sound of his sobs growing as if they were ripping through the thin walls of the confessional, straight through Mancini's soul. With growing agitation, the normally calm priest started to raise his voice as he spoke to the desperate man.

'For the love of the Almighty, just tell me what it is you did. Do you think that you are the only person on earth who has sinned? We are all sinners; we have all had to beg God for forgiveness at one time. Tell me, tell me what you did.' But, despite the priest's rising impatience the man continued to weep, his words becoming quieter as he tried to speak.

'Surely Father, any sin you have committed would be insignificant compared to what I did to my brother.' Mancini had heard enough; it was time to play his trump card. This, after all, was not about the wreck of a man on the other side of the confessional, it was about him, it had always been about him. He spoke the words in a cold unsympathetic tone now, the gloves were off.

'Either you tell me, and tell me now, or I will walk out of the booth and leave you to the wrath of your brother's spirit. It is your choice; it no longer matters to me. Confess and be free or don't and be damned for an eternity.' Brendon was shocked to hear the words spoken so harshly by the priest, but now he finally realised that he had no choice.

'I, I was responsible Father, it was me who killed my brother.' Mancini placed his ear to the grill; the words Brendon spoke were said so softly that they floated off into the stale ancient air of the church as the desperate priest tried to grasp them.

'So, you murdered your brother, that is what you are telling me?' The priest was smiling now. This was what he wanted to hear; this was his salvation. But he was taken aback by Brendon's quick and forceful response.

'No, No, Father. I mean I was indirectly responsible for

his death. I went on a rare visit to see my parents that weekend, but he was in the house alone. We argued, the way we always do, I said things that I now bitterly regret. I stormed off and told him that he was nothing to me anymore. I said that I was finished with him for good. Oh God, Father, I even mentioned that I hoped that the next time he tried to kill himself then he would have the guts to finally do it.' Brendon was crying now as he continued to speak. 'I didn't mean it, he just made me so angry at times. I'm sure he walked to the loch and committed suicide shortly after I left. So, you see, it was partly my fault.' Mancini had grown silent now. He had not been told what he wanted to hear. After a few seconds, Brendon spoke again. 'Are you ok Father? Will you absolve me of my sins now? I've told you what I did. I am ashamed, yes, but I didn't mean for him to kill himself.'

Suddenly the priest was on his feet, almost laughing with rage. He burst out of his part of the confessional and dragged the curtains apart that shielded Brendon on the opposite side. His face was purple with psychotic anger as his large hands grabbed the shocked confessor by the arms and pulled him out of the booth.

'You stupid idiotic excuse for a human being. You have no idea, absolutely no clue what any of us are capable of. You didn't murder your brother and his ghost is not following you. It doesn't exist, except in your pathetic imagination. Damn you and damn your brother, you both deserved each other.'

Mancini was screaming the words now, spittle spraying over the shocked man he held close to his face. Brendon tried to push the enraged priest away, but his opponent was a much bigger man and of course, he had God on his side.

'What the hell, get off me you, crazy mad man. What the fuck is wrong with you?' Brendon screamed the words as Mancini suddenly used all his strength to drag the confessor to his feet. He swung him around to face the empty pews that stretched in front of them and into the distance of the massive church. The enraged priest held Brendon's shoulders and made him look at the rows of silent wood-panelled benches.

'Show me, go on show me where your brother sits. The place is empty you spineless excuse for a….' The priest and the confessor suddenly stopped shouting as they stared in shocked silence at the old lady sitting alone on the front bench. She blended in perfectly with the crumbling dust-filled church. Her very bones melting into the ancient wooden seats. Her face was as old as time itself. Rotting skin folding over the protruding skull, dead teeth moving slowly, so slowly to speak the words. Words that crawled with the insects through the dust towards Mancini. The priest was on his knees now, his face white with fear and guilt. There was no confessor, there never had been. It was always about him; it had always been about him.

'It is time to join me now Fransesco. It is time for you to

walk with me into the eternal damnation of the night. The Lord has judged, and you know he cannot forgive you. Why should he, when he is the one who understands that we two must always be together? Come now my child, the time has come.' The rotting corpse slowly stood up and crept towards the weeping priest. Its bony arms outstretched ready to embrace Father Mancini. He glanced desperately back at the confessional as the black cloud enveloped his soul and pulled him towards his grave.

If only there had been a priest available. Maybe he could have confessed his sins and been forgiven.

Memorial

This stone is not who I was
This tomb is not what I became
Remember me not for this cold rock
But see me as one who loved and lived and smiled

This heart once beat like yours
This shadow once followed the sun
Think of me as you walk by to tend to your recent dead
And leave me one last flower to show that I am not forgotten

First Love

It is with a mixture of fear, trepidation, and excitement that I finally close the pages of this diary. I will leave it to you dear reader to work out what happened next. I shall not write another word in this book once I leave my old room today. Of course, I could not expect you to read every page written by a tortured rambling teenager. I feel embarrassed now when I look back at some of the stuff I first penned when I was fifteen.

To help you understand why I have reached this point and what I must now do I will highlight only the pertinent parts that relate to my tale. In other words, I have taken out everything in my diary except the bits that talk about her. This is the story of Rebecca, Rebecca Crosby the first girl I ever fell in love with. Was she real or just a figment of a frustrated teenager's overactive imagination? The woman of my dreams or my nightmares? The mysterious girl who I still believe once lived next door. At last, after so many long years I will finally be able to lay her ghost to rest.

Sunday, November 2nd, 1975

I hope they give me money for my birthday next week. Jesus, Sixteen and still I've never even spoken to a female. Well, that's not completely true, old Gideon the maths teacher is female, well I think she is. Oh, and the old bats who serve out lunch, they might be women too, not sure though. No wonder I never meet anyone, why the hell do I have to go to a boy's school? Anyway, money, please, please give me money. I bet my father will come up with some nonsense about buying me books or getting piano lessons. Mum knows I want money, here's hoping she talks him around. School tomorrow, fucking dreading it as always. Stuck up here in this room studying every night, boring, boring, boring. I need to get to university though, It's my ticket out of here. I wonder who the new neighbours next door will be. I bet it's another couple of old codgers, no one else would have the money to buy such a big house. Who else would want to live in this lifeless old lane of fading mansions? Why the hell won't my father give me money, the old moaner has enough of it. Jesus, he is a stingy old goat at times. I think I used to like him at one time, not sure when that was though.

Tuesday, November 11th, 1975

Well, I have to admit, this has been my best birthday yet. Ok, I must go back to school tomorrow but at least I had today off and that just leaves three days until the weekend. Jesus, my dad even stopped moaning for twenty-four hours. It was mum who talked him into letting me dodge school for the day, she is a star. The best bit was that she also took the day off from the surgery and brought me breakfast in bed and my cards. No, actually that was not the best bit. The best part was the old goat having to go to his work. He probably moaned his way through the day while operating on some poor old patient. If I found out I had some horrible disease I would prefer my mum as the doctor rather than him.

Did I say that was the best part? Well I exaggerate, the best part was I got money. Twenty fucking pounds of the lovely stuff. Mum got me the new album from Led Zeppelin and made me laugh when she said that dad had tried to insist that they get me some classical rubbish instead. I think he just says these things to try and annoy me. Yes, despite him, it's been a great day.

Oh, one last thing before I go to sleep. An exciting development with the house next door. A big car pulled up during the afternoon. Mum says the place has been sold so I watched what I assume was the new people arrive from the attic window upstairs. It was getting dark and was not easy to see much. As expected, even in the shadows they looked old and boring as they walked along the path. The trees and bushes are now so overgrown that it was really hard to make them out. Anyway, the best bit. In fact, cancel the money or my dad being away today as the best part of the day. It was the girl. I kid you not, they had a girl in the middle between them as they left the car. I could just make out her shape as she disappeared in the gloom. It was difficult to tell her age, but she at least looked like a teenager and had long dark hair. Maybe life in Priory Lane is looking up. Oh God, I hope she is nice, maybe I could even get to know her. At last, someone has arrived who is not part of the walking dead. A person under fifty in this row of crumbling ancient houses at long last.

Saturday, April 24th, 1976

My decision to move into the attic to study has paid off, but not in the way I expected. Ok, diary, the boring stuff first as I realise, I've not written anything for a few weeks. My final O-level exams start in less than a month and I will admit that I'm beginning to panic. Trying to revise in my room was proving to be impossible with so many distractions. So, as I mentioned some weeks back, I decided to move into the empty loft on the roof of the house. Don't get me wrong, there is loads of crap stored up here, but it does not have a record player, albums, or easy access to my dad's pile of dirty books he hides behind the boiler in one of the spare bedrooms. How funny it would be if mum found them but then again, maybe not. Also, it would take away my only chance of seeing a naked woman.

Or that is what I thought up until today. Do you remember late last year I mentioned the girl who had moved in next door? Well oddly she seemed to disappear or according to my mum, she never existed in the first place. Dad went around to say hello to the new neighbours just after they moved in. He came back with his tail between his legs and said they were very strange and rather unfriendly. I wanted to say, no wonder when they got to meet you, but I thought better of it. When I asked him about the daughter, he told me to stop talking nonsense as they said they have never had children. Well either he is lying, or they are because this afternoon I saw her again for only the second time ever. I reckon I am in love.

Sunday, April 25th, 1976

Damn it, I think I could be in trouble. Not only that, I'm now really spooked out with this whole strange girl thing. Yesterday I could see her through the skylight window sitting alone on a deckchair in the overgrown garden next door. Although she was quite far away, I could still make out her shape and she looked really pretty. She was wearing a short black dress and despite being side on I could make out her long black hair and beautiful pale skin. I watched for hours and must admit it meant I got very little studying done. So much for my good intentions.

And now the bit where I screwed up. Early this morning

I came up with the bright idea to leave the skylight window open by just a few inches. Worse than that I sneaked into dad's study and pinched his binoculars. I did not mean any harm but just thought that on the off chance she was out again then I might get to really see what she looked like close up. It has been unusually warm for April and I hoped she might make another appearance. By lunchtime, I had given up as there was no sign. I went down to get something to eat and came back up around two in the afternoon.

And now the weird bit. She was back sitting in the same position only this time she seemed to be sunbathing and was wearing a bikini. I tried the binoculars but must admit it made me feel weird to be spying on someone who thought they were out of sight. Ok, I admit I had a quick glance and boy is she gorgeous. I decided to not look again and get on with my studies, but I just could not get her out of my mind. If only I had not looked that one more time, but I did. I peered out of the skylight and she was in the same place but sitting facing me. I swear to God that it was as if she was looking straight at me. Perfectly still, perfectly formed. I just could not take my gaze off her face and then the worst thing imaginable happened. The old guy who must be her father was suddenly standing behind her. I don't know where he came from, but he was pointing up at the attic and me. Of course, I ducked down and beat a quick retreat back to my bedroom downstairs. How the hell did he know I was watching his daughter? Maybe she saw me and told him. Oh God, I feel like such an idiot.

I promise, promise, promise, sweet Jesus that I will never ever look into that garden again if you just let me off this one time. I just know the doorbell is going to ring and that old creep from next door will accuse me of watching his daughter. Dad is going to kill me, and mum will be ashamed. Like I'm some sort of old peeping Tom who can't get a girl, so he watches them from afar. Oh Fuck, that is what I am.

Friday, July 23rd, 1976

Hello, diary. Sorry, for not writing anything for a few weeks, but I knew I would not have time while we were away on holiday. Spain was great fun and even my dad seemed to be in a good mood for the two weeks. The old moan gave me twenty pounds to add to the money I had saved. It was hard not to laugh when I was sitting drinking beer in that little bar near the train station. It was the only one I could get served in because the waitress Anna took a shine to me. Dad would have gone mad if he knew but I reckon my mum guessed what I was up to.

Anyway, enough of Spanish holiday talk. The weirdest thing happened today. That strange girl next door who I last saw three months ago is back. To be honest I had started to forget about her since the close shave that day when her father saw me spying from the attic window. Well, there she was standing in the doorway of the decrepit old house next to ours. I just caught a glimpse as dad parked the car on our driveway this morning as we returned from the airport. Unfortunately, the trees blocked my view very quickly and by the time I got out of the car to look she had gone. Mum asked me what I was doing looking into the neighbour's garden.

It's that girl next door, the one you and dad say you have never seen. She was standing in the doorway; did you not see her?

Mum looked at me and laughed before winking and saying, *I thought it was just in Spain that you had a beer?* I told you that she knew what I was up to. She promised not to tell dad so long as I did well with my exam results though. They are due next month. I await with trepidation and dread even though I think I might have done ok.

So, she is back again. From the glance I had this morning she looked beautiful. Tall, slim, long dark hair, just perfect. I'm going to give her a name. Let's call her Rebecca, yes Rebecca Crosby as that is what my father said their surname was. They are a strange family. My parents have given up trying to be friendly as they rarely see them outside their house. No wonder the garden is so overgrown. I wonder how they ever managed to have such a gorgeous daughter. He looks like the Frankenstein monster from those old black and white films, only smaller and older. She just looks ancient. All stooped and crooked. They must have had Rebecca very late in life. Maybe she is adopted or even better, they kidnapped her from some lovely family, and it will be me who comes to her rescue. She will fall at my feet and beg me to take her away with me.

Anyway diary, I need to sleep. I shall dream of the girl next door even if no one seems to believe me that she exists. I wonder when she will appear again. Maybe one day I will get to talk to her.

Monday, August 16th, 1976

Well, what a day, what a fucking great day. Sorry for the swearing diary but needs must. I'm absolutely buzzing! Do you want to know why? Well, even the thought of returning to school this Wednesday cannot ruin my glorious day. I mean I thought Friday was brilliant when my O-level exam results came, and it was, oh yes. The fact that dad has promised to pay for driving lessons on my Seventeenth birthday in November and buy me a car just added to the brilliance. I have to admit I'm starting to think the old moan is not so bad after all. Mum is still my favourite adult though, by a long chalk.

Anyway, I bet you are desperate to know why I am so happy. Well sit back and listen dear diary and I shall give you the news. I had to check back to see when I last mentioned Rebecca and it was nearly a month ago on the day we returned from holiday. Well, this morning around ten I took the coffee and porridge mum made me for breakfast and went to sit at the table outside. Not the one beside the kitchen, I mean the rotting old table near the fence at the end of the garden. I know you are going to think I'm nuts, but I swear to God that this happened. As I sat there, I could hear someone whispering through the trees that border the house next door. It is now so overgrown that it's almost impossible to see through the bushes and shrubs that are taking over. It was difficult to make out exactly what was being said or even if it was a human voice. Despite the warm summer sun, the wind was rustling the leaves and gently vibrating the branches. Ok, I really do feel stupid writing this, I know you will think I have an over-active imagination, but it sounded like, *Peter, Peter, it's me, your girl it's Rebecca. I am lonely, so lonely. Please tell me you love me.* The words sounded so sad, so forlorn but also so beautiful. A soft feminine voice, it was as if the trees themselves were speaking.

Of course, I put it down to my imagination at first but when she spoke again, I went over to the fence. This is the part where you will have to apologise for ever doubting me. Pinned to the top of one of the fence posts was a note. A small damp piece of paper that had been left just for me. I shouted her name into the jungle of overgrown greenery, but I knew she had gone. The note, well you will have to wait until tomorrow as I do not have time to write anymore. All I know is, I'm in love. Is that crazy? Infatuated with a girl I've never met. The truth is I've hardly even seen her except at a distance. All I know is that she is prettier than my cousin June, more lovely than my sexy aunt Rita, and more classy than the girls who hang about the shops in the village, but most importantly, she is mine, all mine.

Tuesday, August 17th, 1976

My best mate Stuart came round on his bike to see me this afternoon. It was good of him to visit as Dunlegan village is a good few miles outside of our boring little town. Anyway, he stayed for a few hours, but I think he sensed that I wanted him to go after a while. No doubt we will end up in some of the same classes tomorrow as he is taking maths and chemistry Highers as well. I was desperate to tell him about Rebecca but somehow, I knew he would not believe me. The lucky bastard goes out with Jenny Hamilton from the town. I will admit she is gorgeous but nowhere near as pretty as my Rebecca. Oh yes, sorry diary, you are desperate to hear what she had written on the note. Ok, well this is what it said.

Dear Peter,

I know you have been watching me from the attic window on the roof of your house. It's ok, I don't mind. I'm really sorry about that time my father saw you watching me. I was so sad when you disappeared. When I can I often go out into the garden in the hope you will be there. Sometimes it can be very difficult as my parents are rather strict about what I do. You see, I have a rare genetic disorder and need to be careful when I am outside the house. Even the slightest knock could cause me a serious problem, so I must stay inside. My private teacher and helpers come to our home as I rarely venture any further. It is not my poor parent's fault; they are doing their best but sometimes I wish I had more freedom.

I hope this does not make you think any less of me. Other than that, I'm a perfectly normal girl. I turned Sixteen last January and my mother and father held a small party for me. It was full of old aunties and uncles, not a handsome boy to be seen. I wish you had been there even though I hardly know you. I hope you don't laugh at me but sometimes I watch you as well from my bedroom window using my father's old binoculars. Please write back and leave your note pinned to the top of the same fence post by Thursday evening. If you don't wish to get to know me more then you do not need to reply.

Regards and Fond kisses, your girl, Rebecca.

I know, I know, how could her actual name turn out to be the same as the one I gave her? I don't understand the coincidence either, but I don't care. It must be our destiny to meet, it is written in the stars. I shall write my note tomorrow when I get back from the torture of my first day in fifth year at school. Best not to pin it to the fence though until Thursday afternoon just in case one of her weird parents finds it. Did I tell you I'm in love? I have a girlfriend now, a real one. Not one of those women who pose in my father's hidden books. I love you, Rebecca Crosby.

Tuesday, October 19th, 1976

I can't believe that it's been more than two months since I last wrote in this diary. But then how could I, my life has been a whirlwind of utter joy these last weeks. I now realise that I must find the time to document what is happening to me so that one day I can look back and relive it all again. Maybe me and Rebecca might even be married by then and we can laugh about our endless notes to each other. Tonight, is the night. It's just after six in the evening, I shall try to do some studying and mum has brought my dinner upstairs on a tray. I know it's going to be impossible to concentrate. There are exactly one hundred and twelve minutes to go until I finally get to meet her, touch her, maybe even kiss my darling, Rebecca.

I think I should fill you in dear diary on what has been happening. After that first note from Rebecca, I left my reply on the top of the fencepost as agreed. Since then we have gone back and forth with letters and I've got to know her so well. We would also agree on a time every few days to see each other through our attic windows. It has been difficult as her parents are very strict and keep a watchful eye on everything she does. The best time for us to see each other is at the weekends when it's light. Unfortunately, our houses are so far apart and separated by trees that she is little more than a shape in the distance. I can only catch a glimpse of her head and shoulders and being so far away she seems so still and lifeless. Last week my darling Rebecca attached a photograph taken last year. She is so lovely and has such a great smile. I've been begging her to meet me one evening at the garden fence but each time I ask she has had a reason why it would be impossible. I was becoming so frustrated with the whole thing that in my last note I implored her to take a chance so that we could talk face to face. I found her reply taped to our fence post last night.

My darling Peter,

I can sense that you are becoming annoyed with me for not meeting you in the garden. I would hate for you to feel bad about me or even start to think that I do not love you. My parents, carer, and teacher seem to be around all the time. That is why even seeing you from the window can sometimes be difficult. But this is all about to change. My mother and father are leaving tomorrow morning for an art show. Did I tell you that they are both painters? My father sells really well, or at least he did when he was younger. My mother paints but I think her work is only tolerated because of my father's success.

So, Kate, my carer will be the only one with me tomorrow evening once my teacher leaves. If it is ok with you, can we meet at the fence at eight p.m.? By then it will be dark and there should be little chance of us being seen. Kate will be clearing up after dinner at that time and I am supposed to be studying. We can talk, even if it's just for fifteen minutes. I am so excited to finally see you, my love. Please tell me you will still think me as lovely as you say in your notes when you see me in the flesh. You make me feel so happy; you are my first and only love. Until tomorrow, sweet kisses. XXXXX

Oh my God, it's now five past seven, how time flies when you are besotted. Fifty-five minutes to go. I shall leave at a quarter to eight by the kitchen door. The last thing I need is for dad to stick his nose in and ask what I'm up to. When I write tomorrow, I will have at long last met my beautiful Rebecca in the flesh. I love her so much that I want to get down on one knee and ask her to marry me. Does that sound stupid? Well, I don't care; I'm in love and it is the greatest feeling I have ever known.

Wednesday, October 20th, 1976

It's fucked, everything is fucked, my life is fucked, I fucking hate, hate, hate my life. I'm still in bed and it's nearly midday. Mum called from her work and I had to get up to answer the phone, that is the only time I've been out of this bed. I shall never go outside again. I wish my life was over. My life is over, fuck this. I hate the world, I hate me, I hate everything.

Saturday, November 6th, 1976

It has been more than two weeks and only now can I bring myself to write about what happened that evening. I can finally see that I let a stupid infatuation take over my world and I feel like a complete and utter idiot. If I ever want to get out of this boring little dump of a town then I need to get my act together and get on with my studies. Anyway, it's my seventeenth birthday next week and dad has already arranged to get me driving lessons. I'm sure he is planning on finally buying me that car he promised, I don't even care what kind it is. Maybe it will even make me more attractive to the opposite sex so I can stop thinking about Rebecca once and for all.

I still shake with a mixture of embarrassment and horror when I recall that evening. Unfortunately, mum was in the kitchen as I tried to leave to go into the garden just before eight. I could tell she was wondering what I was up to going outside at that time on such a damp evening. She asked me if I had started smoking! I eventually convinced her that I just wanted some fresh air and finally escaped but it was now ten past eight. I recall Creeping slowly over to the fence in the dark. The sound of the rain bouncing off the leaves made it an unpleasant walk. I was terrified that she might not have been able to come or worse, made it and then left assuming I had backed out.

I approached the post we leave our notes on. The fence is over five feet high and as I'm only six inches taller; it's difficult to see over. I called her name and I swear her answer sounded exactly the same as the voice I first heard back in August. *Peter, Peter, it's me, your girl it's Rebecca. I am lonely, so lonely. Please tell me you love me.* The words sounded so sad, so forlorn but also so beautiful. A soft feminine voice, it was once again as if the trees themselves were speaking.

I could feel her presence on the other side of the fence. A shadow even darker than the night moving between the small gaps in the wood. I was desperate to see her face and tried to look over the top. It was then that I could feel her hand reaching to touch mine. But it wasn't the smooth skin I expected. With mounting horror, I could feel the bony fingers, the cruel hard grip of hate crushing me. And then I saw the old woman looking up, grinning through her dirty rotten teeth. It was Rebecca's mother who was crouched there in the bushes. I remember running, desperately trying to escape from the horror. I spent the next few days off sick. I told mum I had a stomach bug. I could tell she was worried about me as she mentioned I looked as white as a ghost.

I need to forget about the girl next door now. Her parents are fucking weird, who the hell would do something like that? Did Rebecca set me up or maybe they found out about the plan for the two of us to meet? Either way, I need to finish this once and for all. I wish I could get her out of my head.

Friday, Feb 18th, 1977

I don't know why but after nearly four months of not mentioning her, she is suddenly on my mind again tonight. I suppose with so much happening since that horrible experience with her crazy mother, it has been easy for me to want to forget about Rebecca.

I'm really worried about dad. Yes, I know that anyone reading this diary will think that I don't love him, but the thing is, I do. I desperately hope that I pass my driving test tomorrow morning, just to make him proud. If I do then I will take him out on Sunday in the Morris Marina he bought for me. Well, so long as he is well enough to get out of bed.

If I'm being honest, I have to admit that Rebecca has been pushed to the back of my mind since Stuart split up with Jenny Hamilton. He seems to have a new girlfriend every month, he really does have the gift with women. I do owe him an apology though; I did think he was kidding me when he said that Jenny talked about me a lot. Who would have thought it, my first real date and it ends up being with the girl that every other boy fancies. I suppose you could say we are officially dating now as last Sunday was our fifth time going out together. She must really like me as she pretended to enjoy Star Wars at the cinema in Dundee even though I could see her nodding off. And yet, was she my first real date? Why do I feel disloyal to Rebecca by saying that?

Anyway, I had better get some sleep. Tomorrow is a big day. I think it must be guilt that is making me think about Rebecca after all this time. I've decided that if I do pass my driving test then on Sunday morning, I will go back to the fence post to see if she has left any notes since that night. It's strange that I've not even seen her in the garden or at the window but then to be fair, I haven't been looking.

Ok, I tried to sleep but here I am again and it's two in the morning. I don't count myself as a religious person, even though mum and dad did make me go to church until I reached fourteen. After that, I started coming up with excuses to dodge it. I think they got fed up trying to force me to attend. Now I wish I had continued with it, maybe dad would have been ok. I've just been kneeling beside my bed praying to Jesus. It felt sort of ridiculous and false, but I had to do something. I'm scared about dad. It sounds really bad; cancer is such an awful thing. Please, God, I mean it, don't take him away from me. I'm sorry for ever moaning about him.

Sunday, February 20th, 1977

I still feel awful. Why can someone not invent an alcoholic drink that does not make you feel so bloody ill the following day? I blame Stuart and that new girlfriend of his, Sammy. She is far too old for him and she drinks like there is no tomorrow. It was good fun though and to be fair Jenny did keep telling me to slow down. It's not every day that you get to pass your driving test. I think mum has forgiven me for being so drunk when I came home last night. Thank God that Jenny walked me back, I think mum was impressed with her. I am as well, I reckon Peter is in love, again.

Dad has been bad today. There was no way that I could have taken him out in the car he got me. Maybe it's a good thing as I doubt, I would have been fit to drive anyway. My head still hurts but I'm starting to feel a bit better. Christ, it's nearly six in the evening and it's school tomorrow. Alright diary, I haven't forgotten my promise. I will go to the fence later this evening. I need to find out what happened to Rebecca once and for all.

Tuesday, February 22nd, 1977

It's taken me from Sunday until today to get my head around all this. I know I must get my focus on studying for these bloody higher exams in May. The thing is, if I do well and get A's or B's then there is every chance of me getting into Dundee University this year rather than having to do a sixth year at that bloody school. Come on Pete, get your act together man, you can do this.

I think it is worrying about dad that is getting in the way, well that and Jenny who wants to see me all the time. No, diary, I shall be honest. You know me too well now after all these years of sharing my innermost secrets. It's her, it's

Rebecca who is stuck in my head. It's her who is stopping me from concentrating on my studying. Why did I go back to the fence? I should have left things as they were.

Despite feeling like shit on Sunday, I went out in the dark at around eight to the fence post. I will admit I was spooked, I kept imagining that her crazy old mother might still be lurking behind the trees. Creepy old bastard with her bony fingers waiting to grab me again. She wasn't of course but there was something unexpected waiting for me. Attached to the usual place was a pile of rotting damp paper envelopes. I counted them and there were at least twenty. But that was not all, oh no, there was more. A small cardboard box was hanging by a piece of string from the fence. It too was soaking wet and started to crumble as I carried it back to my room.

I don't have the time to write down what Rebecca told me in all the notes so I will just highlight a few key parts. Some of them were difficult to read as the rain had smudged the words. The first note was from the day after her mum spooked me and the last was written on Christmas Eve.

Pete, I am so, so, so, sorry. My mother found our notes to each other just hours before we agreed to meet last night. I know she went down to see you but will not tell me what happened. I hate her for doing this to me. Please, Pete, write back or wave out of the attic to me, just so I know you still love me.

* * *

It's been weeks now my darling. Why are you blaming me for how my parents treat me? I know they think it's for the best but without you, life will not be worth living. Please, I beg you, write back. Tell me you still care. I love you Peter; you are my first and only love.

* * *

Ok, I know I must accept that after more than two months you no longer care about me. My heart is broken although I still cannot make myself blame my parents. I tried to reason with them, but they will not budge. My father says that any friendship with an outsider could be enough to give me an infection and maybe even end my life. My carer and teacher have to wear masks and keep their distance. I don't care though; I would die happy just to see or hear from you one last time. This will be my last note. If by the end of Christmas day, you have not replied then I will leave you alone. I am not a fool Peter. I've seen you coming back with that girl, I know you are in love with her and not me. Please, just tell me that I mattered to you, even if it was just for a few short months.

* * *

I'm glad that it was too late to do anything about the notes. I know now that had I read the last one when she placed it on the fence then I would have gone to meet her on Christmas day. This is for the best. I feel closure at last and can get on with my life. Yes, it's a coward's way out but the cruellest thing to do would be to start it all up again when I just want to forget her and move on. She will always hold a special place in my heart though. Rebecca will always be my first true love.

The little cardboard box held just two objects. One was a small white marble statue of a young boy and girl holding each other in an embrace. The other was a damp faded photograph of Rebecca taken last summer. She is on her own in the garden next door sitting on a bench. Her skin is so pale, almost white against the long black hair. Her face looks so sad, so still and forlorn. and yet she still looks perfect, so beautiful. Written on the back of the picture were the words, *Peter, Peter, it's me, your girl it's Rebecca. I am lonely, so lonely. Please tell me you love me.*

The last thing I did was to place the little box with the statue inside back over the wall. Maybe that was the only way I knew to let her know we could never go back. Goodbye, my beautiful lovely Rebecca. You were indeed my first love and always will be.

Wednesday, March 7th, 1984

Have eleven years passed since I was that love-struck boy of 17? It feels so strange to write in my diary now, almost as though I am intruding on the life of a forgotten stranger. For a few years, I felt guilty that I stopped writing on that Sunday in 1977 after I found Rebecca's notes. Looking back and reading my history I can understand now why I did. That was the point my life changed, and I was not a child anymore. Maybe I could sense what was coming. The world was no longer about me; it was about my place in the world.

Since then my dear father has passed away and I've lost touch with all my old friends including Stuart and Jenny. I did make it to university and the escape to freedom I always dreamed of. So far, I have never married or really been in love again. Life somehow now feels empty and unfulfilled despite achieving what I thought I wanted. Maybe I miss that boy who was able to look forward to what was coming rather than back at what could have been. How I wish I could return to the days when I lived in my own little innocent cocoon protected by two loving parents. I miss my dad so much.

Mum is downstairs with various aunts, uncles, and friends. Everyone is mucking in to help with the house move. It's sad to see so much history, so many memories going into the skip or the bonfire in the garden. I know she is only being practical as her new flat is so small compared to this place. Even now, ten years after my father passed away, it feels wrong to throw most of his stuff out. I can see my uncle Francis through the bedroom window, he looks so much like my father. I am sorry to tell you this dear diary, but once I have written this entry you too will be going into the inferno of dead memories. How embarrassing it would be if anyone opened these pages.

I was meant to find this old book and read it as I now understand what I must do. On the rare occasions in the last ten years that I visited I have never once looked into my old room. Mum had cleared most of my stuff into boxes in the attic anyway. The house next door has been unoccupied for at least five years and now lies even more overgrown and derelict. Mum told me that the old woman passed away first and was quickly followed by her partner. She also reminded me that the daughter they supposedly had never existed. Did I imagine that Rebecca was a real person? I searched the boxes in my room for evidence of her notes but there was nothing. And yet dear diary, you do not lie. This morning while I was helping to clear the garden, I found the statue of the young boy and girl embracing. It was embedded in the mud on our side of the garden. I have no doubt that it was thrown there not long after I had returned it that final night.

So, on this penultimate day in our old house, I shall finally find out the truth. Tonight, when my mum and any visitors who are staying are asleep, I shall break into the house next door. There will surely be something to tell me you existed my lovely Rebecca. I hope you found your freedom be it in life or death. Maybe once I know you really existed then hopefully, I too can discard the memories and finally start to live again.

* * *

The cold brittle chill clings to the hills and forests that surround the small affluent Scottish village of Dundornan. The winter night has fallen over the tree-lined streets of large old mansions while the few streetlamps fight a losing battle with the murky gloom. It is now two a.m. and just one light shines from the massive homes on Glendinny Road. It's coming from one of the upstairs windows of Torveen House. It's the one halfway along the lane, you can't miss it, it's next to that crumbling overgrown mansion that was vacated some years ago.

The light is suddenly extinguished and a few minutes later a hooded male figure creeps out of the back door. He has a small torch in his left hand and a claw hammer in the other one. Slowly he moves towards the old wooden fence that separates Torveen House from the building he intends to break into. He drops the implements onto the other side and hauls himself over into the rambling bushes and overgrown grass of the neighbouring garden. The man has blackened his face with boot polish and wears dark clothing and gloves. You can sense by his demeanour that he is a man with a purpose. Nothing is going to stop him. He is on a mission to lay the ghosts of the past to rest no matter what it takes.

The door at the front of the house is solid and will not budge. Trying to break it down with the hammer will be sure to attract attention even in the depth of night. The figure moves stealthily around the perimeter of the building checking each window. *Surely one of them will be either unlocked or broken after all this time?* A feeling of frustration is starting to envelop the figure as it finally reaches the back door of the building. Suddenly a crashing sound followed by cursing rents the still night air. The man has fallen over a filthy plastic bin full of rotting waste and foul-smelling water. He picks himself up and stands still for a few minutes, straining to hear if he has attracted any unwanted attention. The night remains as it was before, silent and deep. He tries the door and like every other part of the house, it is tightly barred against any intruders. There is nothing left to do but go for it. He raises the claw hammer and sends the glass splintering into thousands of little shards across the inside of the hallway.

It has only taken him ten minutes to explore the lower floor of the house. He has no interest in anything other than finding proof that his beloved Rebecca ever existed. The building is succeeding so far in keeping its secrets. Each room has been furnished exactly the way you would expect of an old couple on the final run towards oblivion. Damp rotting patterned carpets, oddly assorted ornaments covered in cobwebs and grime, and stained photographs of the long-dead family. Not one of them shows the girl he is searching for. Various paintings lay scattered around along with brushes and pots. Nothing to even hint that a beautiful young woman ever lived here. But he is not surprised. The man shines his torch towards the foot of the stairs. He knows that the upper floor is where she lived and breathed. That will be the place that will finally prove that their love was real.

His confidence is starting to wane as he shines the torch on the fourth door. The first three rooms on the upper floor have been disappointing. One a foul-smelling black stained bathroom with a bath full of stagnant water, the next looked as though it has been used to store junk, and the final one was obviously the old couple's bedroom. A multitude of old rags and patterned blankets adorn the small double bed, the floor covered in discarded dirty clothes. There are now only three doors left and a small stairway up into the attic.

The man stares towards the end of the beam. The light has focused on the only thing in the room. A small porcelain doll is perched on an ancient wooden chair. It is still dressed in the clothes of a toddler, the pale blue eyes fixed on the intruder. A feeling of dread is starting to permeate his body. Everything looked normal until he entered this room. Now the first stirring of doubt is creeping into his soul. He turns around and closes the door behind him. The man is no longer so sure-footed, his sense of purpose is diminishing as he questions whether he should continue with his quest.

The penultimate room holds what he feared it would. Another porcelain doll is sitting on a carbon copy of the ancient chair that he discovered next door. This time it is larger and looks like it's supposed to be a child of ten or eleven. Its long dark hair has been twined into a ponytail and in its outstretched arms, it holds a copy of the book, 'Alice in Wonderland.'

The intruder moves quickly to the final room. His nerves are taught, and his heart is beating heavily. A sense of dread and disappointment is overwhelming him now. He feels sick, sweat is running down his face. *You fool, you stupid fool. You let this old pair of devils lead you a merry dance all these years.* The final room brings what he expects. This time the doll is almost life-size. Its pale legs nearly touch the floor as they dangle over the edge of the old chair. The face and torso resemble a teenager. It wears cut-off denim shorts and a t-shirt. The long black hair now covers its face, but he can still see the penetrating blue eyes mocking him.

He finally understands and realises he has seen enough. The man starts to walk towards the staircase and escape.

The stale smell and filth are becoming too much. And yet he hesitates. The truth is all around him, but he still holds onto a glimmer of hope. Years and years of guilt and belief have been almost crushed. *Why not climb up into the attic Peter? You have come this far; you might as well see it through. Clear up any doubt once and for all.*

You can see the beam of the torch change direction in the deep black hallway. It is now pointing at the stairs up to the final room in the roof of the crumbling old house.

He can't move, it's as if his body has closed down and frozen to the spot. His blood has turned to ice and his horrified eyes stare transfixed at the scene. There is an old settee, just big enough for the three figures that sit looking back at him. The beam of the torch is fixed on the porcelain dummy seated in the centre. It is Rebecca, exactly how he remembered her. She is wearing the black dress and the pale colour of her perfect skin is accentuated by her deep blue eyes and long black hair. She sits rigid and proud despite the two rotting corpses that have melted into either side of her. He is sure that he can see a tear sliding down the side of her smooth white cheek.

He is turning now, dragging his eyes away from the beam of the torch. His feet are moving towards the door and freedom. His fingers grip the handle as he pulls it open to make his escape. This is his last chance to finally break free of the guilt and live his life in reality at long last. Behind him, the figure has already started to stand up. The rotting bodies of the long-dead couple on either side of Rebecca are stuck to her dress. They move in unison with her until the decayed bones and flesh crumble around the porcelain figure as it stretches its long arms out towards the escaping beam of the torch. *Peter, Peter, it's me, your girl it's Rebecca. I am lonely, so lonely. Please tell me you love me.*

The man drops the torch and falls to the floor, the light flickering and then going out. He covers his face with his hands so he cannot see what is floating toward him in the dark. At last, at long last, he will finally feel the touch of his first love. The one love that you can never forget.

Concrete Ghosts

Our youth is measured in monuments we remember whether people
or stone
Mine was nine graceful arches of concrete with words carved and
spirits of lost friends
Time does not stand still but your beauty always did
A lonely sentinel whose tall shadow befriended our childhood
Reduced to dust in a cloud of descending memories
No longer do you own the valley, no more do you await our call
And now like falling leaves, we join you one by one
An arch for each soul to become your concrete ghosts.

Floodland

The eleven carriages of the London to Glasgow train snakes its way through the low hills of Cumbria. The red machine seems to glide along with minimal effort almost as though the rising gradient and driving rain are having little impact. Fifty years previously the scene would have been very different. A massive black steam engine billowing smoke would have been toiling hard to drag its heavy load past the bridges and embankments. The syncopated roar of its pistons echoing across the hills as it struggled to overcome the burden of nature's fury.

It's not just the external panorama that has changed so much during the last half-century. No longer do men in hats sit reading newspapers while slim elegant women struggle to walk to the dining car in their tight skirts and high heels. Gone are the sectioned compartments with fabric cushioned seats and the smell of antiquity. No more can you drowse off to sleep to the clickety-clack of the carriage wheels as they move along the steel rails. Now everything seems so smooth and unexciting. The sleek electric engine can eat up the miles without even a hint of having to work hard. Most of the passengers no longer make the effort to dress up for the occasion. Casual attire dominates as everyone stares into a smartphone or tablet. A traveller from the past would note the change in the shape of many of the passengers. Long gone are the tight skirts, high heels, suits, and newspapers. Everyone now looks well fed but less healthy. Almost as though there is no longer a need to work through life, it is as though life works for you.

The man sitting in carriage E, seat 42A looks no different than any of the other passengers as the train nears the border city of Carlisle. Of course, that is where the human similarity ends, and the internal differences take over. Every single person on the train will have a tale to tell of laughing, crying, winning, losing, falling in love, being lonely, being happy, being sad, and being alive. They will also be aware of their impending death, that thing we try to push to the back of our minds until it finally hunts us down. Each and every one of them may be staring into their phones but all of them are trapped in the cycle of life, just like me and you.

And then there is Mr. Owen Hunter. The main difference between Owen and his fellow travellers is that he is staring out of the window rather than looking into a smartphone. In fact, he does not even carry a phone with him. Now that is what we would consider as being unusual in these days of social media and mass communication. That's the thing about Owen, he has always been different, a rebel without a cause some might say. Or maybe it's just that he is slightly more fucked up than the rest of us. Try not to be smug and look down on him. Can you really see into a mirror and say you have never made a mistake? I know I can't, not by a long way. If you can then I don't believe you. Anyway, Owen Hunter. A man on a final journey that will at long last give him a reason for living, just as the end approaches. Talk about bad timing.

***

Owen watched the streaks of water run down the carriage window as the lush green countryside rushed past. He could feel the train starting to slow down for the Carlisle stop. One more station and he would be back in his birthplace, Scotland. Forty long years had disappeared in a flash since that day in 1982 when he boarded the train to London. Of course, he had always expected to return, go back to Dundee to visit his mother and sister. He never did and now both the city and his family felt like distant memories in his head rather than real people. His sister had visited him a few times in the early years, but his mother never did. He knew that she had felt betrayed by him, leaving so suddenly on a whim to meet a girl he hardly knew. His sibling's visits in the late eighties had petered out as he became lost in a world of drinking and excess. He still occasionally thought about them. His mother would be in her eighties now and probably long gone. Maybe his sister was too. Figures from the past who meant little now, but they still cast a small shadow of guilt and regret over his heart.

For the hundredth time, Owen reached into his pocket to find his phone only to remember he had convinced himself to leave it behind. Cindy had been reticent about him taking this trip in the first place, but she was aghast when he insisted that he would not be taking his phone. 'Owen, for heaven's sake. What if you have an accident on the mountain? How will you get help? And what if something happens to one of the kids or me, how will I contact you? This is stupid, and remember, you're not a young man anymore.' He had only half listened to her. That way couples who have been married for an eternity have of communicating with each other. One talks and the other one hears a voice, but it no longer registers.

'Yes, you're right dear.'

'Right about what? What did I just say, I bet you're not even listening as usual.'

'Yes, you're right dear.'

Owen had shrugged the comments off and kept his fake smile up. The last thing he wanted was to leave London under a cloud, the same way he had left Dundee all those years ago

'You'll be fine Cindy. Just go out with Edith or one of your other friends and enjoy yourself. Christ, you always tell me I'm getting under your feet anyway. And the ones you call kids have their own life now. Jesus woman, we barely see them these days unless they need money or a babysitter. They stopped being real kids years ago.'

It dawned on him that he had not drunk or had anything to eat since leaving London four hours ago. Owen struggled to his feet just as the train pulled into the cavernous dome of Carlisle station. He weaved his way through the outstretched legs and people returning from the toilet to finally arrive at the buffet car. A drunk couple in front of him were trying to buy cans of beer but from the heated discussion, it sounded like the stock had already sold out. Even though he had not touched a drop of alcohol in twelve years he still felt as though he was still part of its culture. One drink might set him back on the path to oblivion but knowing he still had the choice kept him from actually doing it. He could smell the booze escaping from the pores of the drunk couple who finally stormed off with cans of gin and tonic. 'Fuckin joke this train. Nae fuckin beer, whit the fucks that aw aboot, useless prick.' The object of their vitriol, the dining car attendant smiled wearily at Owen.

'What can I get you, sir? Please don't tell me you want a can of beer.' Owen laughed sympathetically at the stressed-out employee.

'Just a white coffee please.'

'I've still got some cans of gin and tonic left if you want

them. I would love to sell them before that pair of drunken idiots come back for more.' Both men laughed and nodded to each other knowingly. The attendant because he felt smug and Owen because he was really one of them, and in his day, he probably would have been much worse.

'You going on a visit to Scotland then or is it business?' Owen felt slightly annoyed that the attendant had the audacity to ask him if he was a visitor to his own country. Even though he had not been north of the border in forty years he still considered himself a true Scot. He took pride in still having a Dundonian hint to his accent even if it had warped into a confused concoction of English and Scottish over the years.

'No, just on a four-day break. I'm going to climb Ben Nevis. Always fancied coming back to my home country with a bang. Not been over the border since I was 20. Now I'm retired I just thought, well why not?' The attendant looked him up and down and raised his eyebrows as though he was a schoolteacher about to administer some wise words.

'Well, you be careful mate. Climbing Ben Nevis is hard even for the youngsters. You want to watch yourself up there at your age. The rains coming and it will be extremely tough, maybe even dangerous.' Owen took his coffee without saying another word. *Cheeky bastard, how old does he think I am?* He suddenly felt more sympathy for the two drunks who had been palmed off with cans of gin and tonic than he did for the man serving him from behind the cramped little counter.

Hundreds of miles south of the speeding train a lone man walked his dog along the sandy beach of Chalkdown, a small Essex coastal village. The early evening gloom was descending as the sea raged violently to his left. No one else was out on a grim day like this but Brian Ettingham was not a man to let a little storm get in his way. He had trodden the same path with his beloved Labrador, Etty countless times over the last 12 years. He would walk in rain, snow, sun and even violent wind, but today something was different. Something was very wrong and as Etty ran to the edge of the rough angry sea he shouted over the storm for her to come back. As he watched her disappear his eyes suddenly focused on the waves. The realisation of what was changing hit Brian just as he lost sight of Etty. The water was moving inwards, but not in the gentle way that the tide does. The North Sea was marching like an army hell bent on destruction. Within seconds just like his beloved companion he too was engulfed in the roar of the ocean as it devoured all in its wake.

* * *

The train had sat motionless in the cavernous Carlisle station for almost an hour now. Inside the carriage, people still chatted and bustled around while stretching their legs or walking to one of the on-board toilets. The only one who seemed to be watching out of the window was Owen. The rest of the passengers had accepted the vague electronic communication that had filtered through the speakers in the ceiling.

Good afternoon ladies and gentlemen, this is your train manager Bill Robertson speaking. Just to update you on the current situation as we head North to our final destination, Glasgow. Unfortunately, we are being held by a red signal here in Carlisle due to a technical issue on the line at Lockerbie just over the border. We hope to have more information regarding our ongoing journey soon. I will update you when I receive further news.

Owen could sense that something was wrong. He watched as water dripped onto the platforms outside even though the station was covered by an impressive Victorian canopy. He remembered checking the weather on the BBC website that morning just before he left his home in London. Despite being nearly the start of summer, the next fortnight had shown nothing but rain. He had pondered calling the whole expedition off but incredibly the weather seemed to improve north of Glasgow. His final destination at Fort William in the shadow of Ben Nevis would be gloomy but dry. Perfect conditions for tackling the long climb. His real worry was if he would ever actually arrive there.

Suddenly Owen caught sight of a large middle-aged man shuffling into the seat opposite his. He felt mildly irritated at the prospect of company. The three seats at his table had been empty since a group of noisy women had exited at Preston. At least they had been amusing as they laughed and shared small bottles of wine between themselves. They were heading out on a hen night in the town and even offered him a drink. Of course, he declined politely without explaining why.

Owen could tell that the newcomer would be intrusive by the way he huffed and puffed as he squeezed into the seat. He placed his large travel bag on the floor beside him and wheezed with the effort.

Carlton Moss was a big man with a big personality, the opposite of everything Owen believed himself to be.

'Bloody trains, so unreliable.' Carlton wheezed some more before continuing in his strong Cumbrian accent.

'If I had known that the damned train was going to be held up, I would have accepted that offer of a lift from Barnaby.' The large man leaned forward over the table towards Owen. He placed his arms almost within touching distance and then held out his hand.

'So, tell me why you are allowing British Railways to take you across the border into enemy territory then? Carlton, Carlton Moss, Border Television executive. You might have heard of me.' Owen deliberately waited a few seconds before shaking the interloper's hand. The man had already irritated the hell out of him with just a few simple sentences. He wanted to reply, *Firstly, it hasn't been called British fucking Railways for decades, secondly, England is the enemy territory to me, not Scotland, and finally, mind your own business you annoying fat bore.*

'Hi, Owen, Owen Hunter. I bet you've never heard of me either?' The sarcasm was not lost on the man who let out an infectious belly laugh. For the first time, Owen felt his guard coming down slightly as he continued. 'Yes, I'm worried about the amount of rain out there. It's been like this since we left London. I wonder if there is flooding and the train might not be going any further?' Carlton eased his large frame back into his seat before letting out another hearty chuckle.

'Oh, we'll be heading into the land of the tattie munchers and bagpipe weavers, I can assure you of that. No one, not even good old British Railways will stop Carlton Moss when he has an important meeting to attend. Anyway, they change drivers here at Carlisle and the new guy will be desperate to get back to Glasgow.' With those very words, the train suddenly jolted forwards and started to move. The journey into the land of the enemy had resumed despite the deluge.

* * *

The faded industrial landscape of Motherwell on the outskirts of Glasgow looked even more ominous in the damp gloom. Despite being an early afternoon in mid-May the panorama outside was one of an impending weather apocalypse rather than the promise of summer to come. Windswept rain was lashing down as the dark grey sky unleashed its venom on the landscape below.

Opposite him, Owen could hear the heavy snores of the supposed Border Television executive, Carlton Moss. The two men had chatted for an hour while the late running train crawled its way north through the rain-sodden fields and hills of southern Scotland. Of course, it had been mainly Carlton who had done most of the talking as he harangued Owen about his prominent role in Border TV and the famous people he knew. Owen had started to doze off until he was suddenly jolted out of his seat as the words the interloper spoke filtered into his brain. 'So, enough about me. Where are you off to this fine weekend? You still haven't told me.' Before Owen could get the first word of a reply out, the man opposite carried on talking.

'I bet you're not going as far as me. Can you believe it, I mean who asks for a meeting in Fort William? The bloody place is absolutely the back of beyond. I have another trip on the awful British Railways again tomorrow to look forward to. Another four hours stuck in this metal tube chugging along through the rain.' Owen sat up more attentively, he had to concentrate to make sure the man opposite did not find out that they were both heading for the same destination.

The last thing he needed was to have to sit and listen to him on another long journey.

'Oh yes, lucky for me. It's just some local hills near Glasgow that I'll be climbing. I'm glad I don't have to travel as far as Fort William. Still, it's nice scenery up that way.' Carlton nodded without enthusiasm and shuffled his large frame in the seat before replying.

'Well, I can't complain too much. The bigwigs at Border Television have put me up in the Central Hotel tonight. It means a nice dinner, maybe a big juicy sirloin steak, a bottle or two of vintage wine and up for the 8.21 from Glasgow Queen Street in the morning.' Owen stared at him in disbelief. *How on earth could so many coincidences happen at once?* Incredibly the so-called famous Carlton Moss was staying in the same hotel tonight as he was. Not only that, they would both be booked on the same train in the morning. There was nothing left for Owen to do but tell a white lie.

'Wow, the Central Hotel, eh. I bet that cost a pretty packet. I'm down with the plebs at the holiday inn, unfortunately.'

Owen looked at the sleeping man slouched opposite him. Even the rain battering off the windows and the chatter of voices around him could not drown out the loud snores emanating from the wheezing lungs of Carlton Moss. Now he had a predicament. He would either need to come clean or spend the evening trying to avoid bumping into his new acquaintance. But, even if he did, Owen knew that the Fort William train was only four carriages and it would be almost impossible to not be seen. *What a fucking idiot I am for not bringing my phone. I could have changed my tickets to a later train tomorrow and just had room service tonight.* There was only one thing he could do. He would call Cindy from the hotel landline and get her to rebook his ticket. So much for disappearing and not needing to stay in communication. Day one of his adventure into solitude and he had messed it up so soon. He could already hear the lecture he would get from his wife. *I told you to take the bloody phone with you. When will you ever listen to me?*

How strange it is that life can be full of such extremities. Here was Owen trying so hard to avoid having to travel with someone he found to be a bore, while outside the world was being turned upside down. The rain was still falling, almost 12 hours now and it was not light rain. It was a torrential downpour. Already the streets were running with water like little streams that now waited desperately to grow and reach adulthood. They dreamed of becoming rivers, lakes, and even oceans. And above them, the dirty black clouds promised to feed the infants so that they could fulfil what nature had always intended them to be. Angry raging torrents hell-bent on eradicating mankind.

* * *

'Cindy, it will be fine. Honestly, you're getting carried away. You need to stop watching those bloody documentaries about global warming.' Owen lay on his bed in the Glasgow Central hotel while holding the room phone close enough to hear his wife but without it touching his face. He could sense the tension in her voice but both of them knew she was over-reacting.

'If you had taken your bloody phone as I told you to then you would have seen the news. I mean, Jesus Christ Owen, most normal people would at least switch on the tv to catch up on things.' He sighed and looked at the lifeless box above the dressing table.

'I told you, Cindy. The whole point of this trip was to clear my head. I don't want to talk to strangers or look at a phone or television. I just want, need four days for me and absolutely nobody else.' He could sense her mellowing and giving in, accepting his eccentricities, or was it his selfishness?

'Ok, Ok, Owen. It's more the kids I was worried about, well the grandkids I mean.'

'Look, Cindy. I'll call you tomorrow when I get to Fort William. I'm sure the rain will have abated by then and the flooding will be over. Can you just do as I asked you and get me on the 11:12 to Fort William instead of the 8:21? I just want to have a longer sleep in the morning. There's no rush as

I'm not climbing Ben Nevis until the day after.'

'Ok, yes I'll call you back at this number once I've booked the ticket.' As always, she had given in to his demands. He suddenly felt a pang of regret for dismissing her concerns about the bad weather.

'Cindy darling, try not to worry about the rain. You know they have to find something to scare people with on the TV news. No doubt tomorrow the sun will be out, and they'll move onto complaining about the government or some other crap.' He could tell by the resigned tone of her voice that she was still not happy but was accepting his comments rather than getting into another discussion.

'Yes, if you say so. I'll call you as soon as I have things sorted out.'

Owen remained on the bed with his head against the pillows as he contemplated the discussion with his wife. He felt no concern at all. Cindy always panicked about things that would never happen. When she mentioned that the news had talked about the Thames Barrier flooding, he wanted to laugh. *The Same old scare nonsense being spread by social media. A bit of rain and localised flooding and the press try to turn it into something that would sell advertising space.*

Outside he could hear the rain pattering against the windows. The forecast for Central Scotland was light rain, unlike Southern England which was getting a real soaking. Owen pondered going out for fish and chips or maybe finding a restaurant. Somehow, he knew that he would do nothing but lay on the bed until he eventually drifted off to sleep. The thought of meeting that fat bore, Carlton Moss was too much. The reality was, he just could not be bothered moving.

The streetlights reflected off the wet roads of Glasgow on this damp May evening. Taxis and busses threaded their way through the puddles as couples hurried towards the doorway of a pub or into the safety of the cavernous Central Railway Station. The rain had little impact on the few people still out as the clock neared 10 pm. Scotland was used to early summer rain, it was used to rain, full stop.

It was different in the little Northamptonshire village of Long Eydon. No one was out and about at this time. A few lights still burned from a handful of scattered houses as worried tenants peered out into the dark at the non-stop deluge that lashed down on the main square. Very soon they would no longer be able to look. Already the normally peaceful River Tove had outgrown its natural home and merged with its sisters. A wall of water was rising as it congregated into a swirling mass determined to find its way to the ocean. The rivers had joined and as one broken through the ancient banks that had always held them in sway. The lights of Long Eydon flickered and died as the roar of nature's destruction devoured all in its wake. The buildings crumbled into the raging angry water taking every shred of human life with them.

* * *

Owen Hunter eventually made it to the dining room at 8:45 in the morning. Having missed dinner, the previous evening he was ready for a hearty breakfast. Of course, we all know that the reason he was late was that he needed to make absolutely sure that Carlton Moss was already on his way to Fort William on the 8:21 from Glasgow Queen Street. He need not have worried. The restaurant was empty except for him and the waitress who led him across the room. 'I can see you are busy; I was lucky to get a table.' The joke washed over the young woman as she pointed Owen towards an empty chair.

'Yes, it has been unusually quiet these last few days. Unfortunately, the flooding across the border has caused a lot of trains to be cancelled. It's pretty scary, did you see it on the news this morning?'

'Yes, well at least they won't need to worry about a water shortage for a while.' The girl gave him an odd look before deciding it was best to end the conversation.

'Tea or Coffee?'

Owen took his time with the sizeable breakfast the girl eventually placed on the table before him. He was in no rush as he still had some hours to kill now that he was getting the later train North. He returned to his room and packed his travel bag before strolling slowly out into the light misty rain.

A large crowd milled around the front of Central Station. A handful of staff in blue uniforms seemed to be trying to placate irate travellers. Unusually for Owen, he decided to find out what was happening and stopped beside a middle-aged couple who stood beside their cases under the ornate station frontage.

'What's the queue for? Is there a problem this morning?' The man looked at him as though he had two heads. He answered in a slightly sarcastic American accent while his wife smirked.

'Where you been the last few days Buddy, Mars?' Owen ignored the comment and waited for the man to continue.

'Flooding. Everything heading South of Scotland is cancelled this morning. You can get as far as Manchester but it's pointless. No flights from Heathrow or Gatwick either. Seems the Thames has burst its banks.' Owen should have felt shocked or at least some form of guilt at not having taken Cindy's concerns seriously. He shrugged his shoulders and without replying to the rude American he walked off towards Queen Street. There was no point in calling her, she would just repeat yesterday's conversation. As far as Owen was concerned the rain would eventually stop falling and any damage would be covered by the insurance companies. His house was on high ground, the worst Cindy would have to deal with was driving the car through a few puddles to get to the shops.

Unlike the station he had just left, Glasgow's second railway terminus had very few people waiting at the entrance. The large glass frontage looked out onto an almost empty George Square. There looked to be more pigeons than human beings willing to brave the dank weather.

It was beginning to dawn on Owen just how different he was starting to feel. He still felt numb as though life was passing him by as he watched like a casual observer from the side-lines. The change was that for the first time in many years he had a purpose at last. No one was going to stop him from doing this, not Cindy, not the kids, and most definitely not some stupid rain shower. Owen Hunter was going to climb to the top of Ben Nevis the day after tomorrow no matter what obstacle was placed in his way. Nothing mattered anymore. It was just him, on his own, and the mountain. This would be the end of his journey. What that meant, he was not sure. He just knew he had to stand at the top of Britain's highest peak and look down on the world below. Prove to himself that he could do something completely on his own. No phone, no companion, nothing but him.

Inside the station was busier than he expected. People milled around dragging wheeled baggage trolleys behind them or stood in small groups staring at the bright display screens while waiting for their platform to be announced. It soon dawned on Owen why there were so many people about. Many of the lines on the screen had, *cancelled due to inclement weather conditions* typed just after the supposed departure time. With growing trepidation, Owen scanned the display for news of the 11:12 to Fort William. A feeling of relief ran through his body as he read the words, *please proceed to Platform 7.*

That would be the end of the good news though. A long queue snaked back from the ticket barrier as people edged slowly towards the six-car train. Without having to ask Owen already knew what the problem would be. The previous train, the 8:21 had been cancelled and now two loads of passengers were hoping to squeeze on board. In the middle of the throng, he could already make out the large frame of Carlton Moss cursing British Railways for being so useless.

Owen stood jammed between the bikes and damp-looking fellow passengers in the space just outside the toilet. Each time someone shuffled through the carriage to use the lavatory everyone including him had to bunch up together to let them go past. There was nowhere else to go as every seat and space was already taken. He knew he had been lucky to even get on board. Many irate ticket holders had been told that the train was full and that they would have to wait at least 3 hours for the next one. It was to be a long journey. Even the pleasure of watching the gorgeous Highland scenery speed by was being denied due to the human throng causing the windows to steam up. All this meant little to

Owen as he waited for the inevitable to happen. With a four-hour journey ahead of him It would only be a matter of time before Carlton Moss came bumbling through the crowd to find the toilet.

The train had hardly reached the outskirts of Glasgow when a wheezing cursing supposed television presenter squeezed himself out of his seat in the next carriage and started to push his way towards the nearest toilet.

Four long hours later the train disgorged its weary passengers onto platform 2 at the compact modern railway station in Fort William. It was hard to believe that it would soon be June as the normally picturesque background of mountains and forests were completely hidden behind a veil of mist and clouds. Owen tried to edge forward through the throng, each step he took being mirrored by the large man following behind him.

'So, the Caledonian hotel you said.' Owen raised his eyes to the heavens before replying impatiently.

'Yes, yes Carlton. I thought I told you that countless times. The Caledonian.'

Owen had to bluff his way through the awkward conversation when the two men had met a few hours earlier. He managed to convince his new friend that he had changed his mind and decided to tackle Ben Nevis instead. Carlton had been delighted to meet him again. He then insisted on keeping him company for the rest of the journey. The two men had stood crushed together while Owen was bombarded with endless tales of famous people as well as the intricacies of being a Border Television executive. As the train slowed or accelerated Carlton would lose his balance and bump into his new-found friend. It had come as a massive relief to Owen when he found out that the strange co-incidences were over, and they were booked into different hotels.

Just before the two men left the station to face the now heavy rain, Carlton turned towards Owen. 'So, you're definitely up for meeting tonight at 7:30 in the Ben Nevis Bar?' Owen tried to hide the guilt on his face as he replied.

'Yes, of course, as we already agreed. I thought you had a meeting to go to though?' Carlton placed his bag on the ground and wheezed.

'Oh yes, erm, don't worry, that'll only last half an hour. I just need to sign off some papers that's all. It's for the Kylie Minogue interview at Border TV.' Owen stopped in his tracks and could not hide the sarcasm in his reply.

'What, you telling me that Kylie Minogue lives in Fort William now?'

The two men said their goodbyes and departed to their respective hotels. Owen could not help feeling that he was not the only one who was lying. Of course, he had no intention of going to the Ben Nevis bar tonight at 7:30 or at any time. An early night and then he would hit the road in the morning. A dawn start on the mountain. Not that in this weather he expected to meet many other climbers.

Carlton Moss remained stationary as he watched the other man hurry through the rain towards the High Street. Once he was sure that Owen was finally out of sight he turned and made his way back towards the platforms. He took out a pencil and a well-used notebook before sidling up to the front of the train. He jotted down the number and then shuffled excitedly over to the next platform. A big shiny black steam engine and a green diesel locomotive sat together on a grass-grown siding glistening in the rain. They were used for the tourist train that ran from Fort William to Kyle of Lochalsh. Carlton jotted down the numbers of both the engines and then sat down on a deserted bench under the station canopy. He had already decided to wait here until it was time to meet his new friend again. There seemed little point in going to his bed and breakfast room to be alone, the way he always was. Anyway, maybe another train would arrive soon, and he could get another number added to his list.

Outside the station, the water was flooding into the drains. The High Street for now still looked the way it always did during a heavy downpour. The same could not be said of the Northumberland Coastal village of Saint Byre. For hundreds of years, it had edged slowly towards the sea as the cliffs eroded and fell before the might of the ocean. The storm had battered the little settlement incessantly during the last few days. And yet nobody could have seen what was about to happen. It was as if the wind, the rain, and the mighty North Sea decided to merge for just one final violent attack. The authorities had told the villagers that they had at least 30 or 40 years left before the cliff erosion would finally eat into their homes. All they knew about their impending doom was a deafening rumbling sound as the cliffs gave way and Saint Byre crashed downwards into a watery grave taking every single villager with it.

***

Owen tried to focus his eyes on the dim light that penetrated the room. Before going to sleep last night, he had pulled the black-out curtains tightly across the window. Despite the dawn breaking through at 5 am and the sound of heavy rain battering off the roof, he had slept like a log. In fact, he had probably the best sleep he had in years. Owen knew why although he hated admitting it to himself. It was because for the first time in so long he had a purpose and no one else mattered. He didn't even care about the incessant rain that had appeared despite the forecast saying it would be dry. Nothing, absolutely nothing was going to stop him from reaching the top of Ben Nevis today. His time had arrived.

The white Skoda taxi splashed through the puddle-strewn road as it pulled up outside the Caledonian hotel.

Owen jumped into the back seat and placed his rucksack beside him. He could make out the back of the driver's head, a mass of ginger curls rolling down his broad shoulders. Owen could see his eyes looking at him through the rear-view mirror as if he was surveying a madman. 'You do realise that the Glen Nevis visitor centre doesn't open until 10, don't you?'

'I don't mind, I'm climbing Ben Nevis today not looking to buy tourist junk or drink expensive coffee.' The driver remained silent for a few minutes before replying. Owen wondered if he had gone too far and offended him. He finally turned around for a few seconds and spoke.

'Listen man. Only an eejit would go climbing today. The mountain will be a washout. Have you not seen the news? Half of England is underwater, it sounds terrible. I think a lot of people have lost their lives in the flooding. You try and climb today, and you will be another one.' Owen shuffled uncomfortably in his seat. He simply wanted the driver to take him to his destination, not give him a lecture. *Bloody hell, I thought I'd left that all behind in London with Cindy. Why don't you mind your own fucking business and just drive, that's what I'm paying you for.*

'It's ok driver, I'm not daft but thanks for the concern. I'm not going to actually climb the mountain today. I'll just go for a small walk and then maybe call you later to pick me up.'

'Better you than me mate. Even the lower paths will be tricky in this monsoon.'

Both men decided it was best not to continue the conversation and the next ten minutes were spent in awkward silence.

Despite the water pouring down the windscreen, Owen could make out the lights of a roadside service station ahead. It dawned on him that he had not eaten since yesterday morning and despite feeling no hunger he knew he had to have something to tackle the climb ahead. 'Sorry, could you just pull into the garage over on the right for a few minutes? I need to get some provisions, thanks.'

The young woman was still in the process of opening the shop and looked surprised to see a customer at 7 in the morning. Owen busied himself picking up chocolate bars and peanuts. He placed them on the counter and then suddenly remembered that he needed water. He hurried back to the fridge and returned with two expensive plastic bottles of the stuff. The irony of buying something that was falling in torrents outside was not lost on either of them. The girl had a worried look on her face, Owen could see fear in her young eyes. He paid without speaking in case he was confronted with more reality and quickly ran back out to the waiting taxi.

It was barely two miles from the centre of Fort William to the visitor centre at the foot of the mountain, but it took

15 minutes to complete the journey. The driver carefully avoided the pools of rain that had swelled into small ponds all over the road. They met no other traffic other than a police car heading in the opposite direction with its blue lights flashing.

As Owen stepped out of the taxi into the deluge the driver made one last plea to him. 'Listen, man, for the love of God don't stray too far up there today. While you were in the garage, I got a call from the wife. The First Minister is holding a nationwide broadcast at 10 this morning. The floods overnight have worsened and are now spreading towards the North.' Owen grabbed his rucksack and made it obvious that he was impatient to be left alone.

'It's fine, as I told you, I only intend to do a small walk and then head back.' The taxi driver shook his head before replying.

'Well, I'm not sure I'll even be able to come back for you. The roads are a mess. I really think you should reconsider and return to Fort William with me now.'

Owen handed him 4 already wet £20 notes and turned towards the track without another word. He knew it was far too much to pay even for an expensive Highland taxi, but he didn't care. Money meant nothing to him now. It never really had. He pulled the waterproof over his head and marched through the wet cobbles and grass towards the start of the path. The lights of the still-closed visitor centre barely penetrated the all-pervading mist and rain. Even though He was at the foot of the great Ben Nevis and walking towards the peaks of the Grampians Owen kept his head down. He knew that he would see nothing today except the earth and rocks under his feet. The mist might finally give way to the dark clouds above, but it did not matter. He wanted nothing at all other than to stand at the top of the mountain, at long last. Then and only then would he feel that he had finally returned to his native land and laid the ghosts of his mother and sister to rest.

The white Skoda nudged its way slowly along the winding road back to Fort William. Inside the driver wiped the ginger curls away from his face. He was still flabbergasted that the man he had dropped off was going out on Ben Nevis alone. Hamish had seen many idiots over the years lose their lives on the mountain, this guy was an absolute certainty to be another. His mobile rang out and he leaned forward to swipe the screen to answer. The sound of his wife crackled through the car speaker. Hamish could not make out what she was saying but he could feel the fear and panic in her voice. *Home, nightmare, Hamish, please, oh God Please, Hamish, Hamish…* The speaker suddenly died but not because she had stopped talking. It was the white Skoda; it had left the edge of the road that had collapsed into the gorge below. Hamish had gone to meet the Gods of the sea.

* * *

It was barely 10 o'clock in the morning and yet Owen already knew that he was in trouble. It was almost impossible to see the track ahead for more than a few feet as the wet mist shrouded everything in a murky deathly white. All around him he could hear running water as small streams built up a pathway to escape down the mountain. The route he had chosen had once been known as the tourist climb as it was considered the easiest way to the summit. Even in good weather, many had given up on the four-hour slog to the top. In the non-stop downpour that Owen faced any hope of making real headway was going to be very difficult.

Each weary step into the squelching mud took our intrepid climber a few feet closer to his final destination. He had cleared out every single thought in his head to allow the voice to talk him into reaching the top. 1,2,3,4, left foot forward, 1,2,3,4, right foot forward, 1,2,3,4…. Cindy, his children, ex-drinking buddies, old work colleagues, his mother, sister, and long dead father, all sacrificed from memory in honour of the God of the mountain that towered above him.

He became aware that the track was narrowing and becoming steeper and rockier. Owen was relieved to leave the mud behind but now came the added danger of slipping on the wet stones. He couldn't see the edge of the track but guessed that it would drop into a chasm and certain death far below.

Owen sat with his back propped up against the rocks. Water was seeping through every layer of his supposed waterproofs, but he no longer cared. When he last had the strength to check his watch, he had been amazed to see that it was now mid-day. He had been struggling through the storm for more than four hours and yet could sense he was still a long way from the summit. The realisation that he would not make it had finally hit him as exhaustion took over. Every fibre of his body felt numb from the cold, every inch was soaked through. He could feel a drowsy acceptance creeping into his soul. *Was this it? The conclusion of his life's journey. How ironic that as in everything he did, he had only made it halfway to his goal. And yet was that not the way life always ended up anyway? Yes, supposedly it was the journey that counted and not the destination. Even those few times you did make it to the final destination it always seemed like a disappointment once you reached the end anyway.*

Owen could feel his body sliding down off the rocks as the water propelled him forward. A small stream was building up through the boulders of the well-worn track and inching him towards the edge. *Any minute now he would disappear into the chasm. Not only had he failed to reach the top, but the mountain was going to send him crashing back to where he belonged, the very bottom. A failure in life and now a failure even in death.* He closed his eyes for what he expected to be the final time and let the water carry him inch by inch towards the inevitable drop.

Suddenly he stopped moving. Slowly he opened his eyes again and was astonished to see a small hut standing on what looked like a flat patch of wet grass. Incredibly he had found the rescue bothy that stood on a remote ledge halfway up the mountain. Owen summoned the last vestige of strength his aching body could muster and stood up. He crashed through the unlocked door and stumbled onto a small sleeping ledge at the back of the little building. And then, to the sound of the never-ending rain, he fell into the most peaceful guilt-free sleep he had known since he was a child.

* * *

Owen studied his surroundings with confusion. Sunlight was sending a bright orange glow through the open door. It took him a few more minutes to realise that he was still alive as he lifted his arm and looked at the watch strapped to his wrist. He blinked in disbelief and then tried to focus his eyes on the little dial. It was 10 o'clock in the morning, incredibly he had slept for almost 24 hours. It slowly dawned on him that something was very different. And then he realised what had changed. It was not just the warm sun flowing through the window of the little hut, it was the silence. The ever-incessant patter of rain had vanished. He stood up and walked shakily to the entrance.

Outside on the grassy ledge, Owen looked around him in amazement at the panorama that fed into his eyes. Above him, the track stretched upwards towards the distant peak as it basked in the hazy sunshine. The sky was a deep blue, with not a cloud in sight. The sun was hot and within minutes steam was rising from his damp clothes. Down below the earth was still covered in what looked like mist or low-lying clouds. Owen wondered if the rain still fell down in the glen and if maybe he had now climbed above the storm. His eyes caught the shimmer of water floating slightly above the mist a few yards away. He wished he had studied the map or at least done some more research. Owen was amazed to see the small loch that he never knew existed nestled in a ravine halfway up Ben Nevis.

Within thirty minutes he was on his way again. Owen had discarded most of his wet climbing gear including the rucksack. He had eaten the light supplies he purchased from the garage the day before and devoured most of the water. He placed the half-empty bottle into a side pocket for later. *What was the point of saving anything else?* This was a one-way journey now; he had always known that. He washed his face and body in the cold water of the misty little loch and felt alive again. The long sleep and the warm sun had re-invigorated his tired body. Owen now tackled the steep track with a sense of enthusiasm and purpose. Above him towered the peak, tall and proud in the sunshine. Below him a strange almost blue haze covered everything. He could just make out the tops of a few other mountains peering out of the clouds.

How different the earth seemed as he climbed higher and higher. Now the rocks and pools of water were hissing as the sun burned down on them. Owen finally reached the plateau near the top after a few hours. Strange memorials made of rocks piled upon each other and a trig point bordered the well-worn path. At long last, he stood at the summit and surveyed the scene around him as a light wind fought to cool the heat from the sun. To his amazement, he saw that the mist and cloud had crept up higher, almost as if it was following him. The adjacent peaks that had protruded through the cloud when he left the little loch had now vanished. All that was left above the blue haze was the final 300 meters of Britain's tallest mountain. Owen didn't care. He had finally done something just for himself. It seemed fitting that it was only him and the head of Ben Nevis left in sight while the world below trudged its chaotic course.

He sat down and rested his back against a small mound of rocks. Owen felt as if life was seeping back into his veins. Maybe this was all he had needed to do to prove to himself that he was not a failure. He thought about Cindy and the kids, but this time it was with affection rather than obligation. Something had changed because he now wished he had his phone with him and could call his wife. Tell her how amazing it was to be on top of the world, tell her he still loved her. Maybe even ask if the panic about a bit of heavy rain was over.

Owen felt contented as he rested in the warm sunshine and reflected back on his life. It was at this point that he noticed the figure moving just above the misty blue haze some distance away at the start of the plateau. A fellow climber was heading towards him. Owen truly smiled for the first time in years and looked forward to greeting whoever it was. The loner now craved human company after so long in the wilderness. Although he had never admitted it to himself, somehow, he had never made any plans to return down the mountain. It was as if the journey here had been so all-consuming that it had only ever felt like a one-way ticket. Now suddenly he felt so alive. He wanted more of this life, he wanted to go home and live again.

The visitor was coming closer, scrambling slowly towards him. Something about the way the person held himself and his still distant shape aroused a hint of recognition in Owen. The nearer the lumbering figure came towards him the more he thought he knew who it was. *That's impossible, no way could he climb up this high. It can't be, surely not?* But it was. The glow of the burning sun shrouded the figure until it was within hearing distance.

'Owen, Owen Hunter. I thought I might find you up here. It's Carlton, your friend Carlton Moss.' With those words, he held out a hand in friendship and then collapsed in an exhausted heap at Owen's feet.

Owen dragged the stricken man over to the rocks and propped him up as best he could. He pulled off the light rucksack attached to his back and then poured the last remnants of his water into Carlton's mouth. He watched it trickle down his chin and drip onto the stones at his feet. Eventually, the clearly exhausted man started to come around. He looked up at Owen who now cradled his head in his hands. 'I knew I would find you up here. Did no one else survive, is it just us?' Owen looked at him with confusion.

'What are you talking about Carlton, what do you mean no one else?' Even though he asked the question he did not take the words of an obviously tired and confused man seriously. But it was the supposedly confused man who was confused by the other's question. It was becoming clear to Carlton that Owen really didn't realise what had happened. 'We need to get you help to get off this mountain Carlton. Do you have a phone with you, I can try and contact mountain rescue.' Suddenly Carlton started laughing, not a chuckle of mirth but a manic laugh of desperation and fear.

'Oh, Jesus in a hand basket, Owen. You don't know what has been happening, do you? I mean you really don't. Where the hell have you been for the last 24 hours?' Owen looked at him with a sense of trepidation even though he still thought the other man was dehydrated and talking nonsense.

'Look, Carlton, have you got a phone or not? Climbing up here has been way too much for you and I can't carry you down. Anyway, look at the mist coming up towards the plateau. It's getting worse and will soon cover even the top of the Ben. We need help.' Carlton turned and looked in the same direction before speaking.

'Owen, I hate to tell you this but that is not mist. It has chased me all the way up the mountain. I swear to God that it was only the fear of death that got me up here.'

'What the hell are you talking about, Carlton? If it's not mist then what the fuck is it? Pink Dragons.' The other man gave the same manic laugh before looking back at his friend with sadness in his eyes.

'It's water, Owen. It's the sea, the bloody ocean. The world is over. The only reason we are still here is that we are probably the last two people left alive above the water line. It started with the rain and then during yesterday the sea flooded the whole of the land, everywhere, or so the prime minister said. It never stopped, it kept rising It's just luck that I followed you here and started climbing yesterday.'

The whole thing sounded so ridiculous and yet Owen somehow knew it was true. It was dawning on him that the little loch he had found in the clouds had probably been the sea as it crept up the mountain. He stood up and started to walk down the slope towards the rising blue mist. Within a few hundred yards he was at the edge of the ocean. A hazy steam rose off the water as it edged slowly higher.

***

The two men sat huddled closely together. They had climbed to the highest point on Ben Nevis as the water continued to pursue them. It now lapped over the last rocks and was almost touching the heels of their walking boots. Above them, the sun shone in a clear blue sky as a peaceful silence reigned over the earth. It was as if the planet had been cleansed and was now ready to renew itself. Maybe the birds above and the fish in the sea still lived but for the human race, time was almost up.

'So, you don't really know all these celebrities you barked on about all the way through that train journey?' Carlton Moss laughed at his friend's comment, but this time it was a hearty happy laugh. He handed the whisky bottle he had taken out of his rucksack to Owen who took another deep drink of the liquid gold.

'It's your fault, Mr. Moss. All these years being tea total and now you talk me into succumbing to the demon drink once more.' The two men chuckled again as Owen handed the bottle back.

'I hear that it's best to die a drunk man than a sober one. It means you feel more relaxed when you get to the gates of heaven. You know, to be judged by God and his mates.' The water was now up to their knees and time was running out. Owen took the bottle again and had another long drink.

'And the only reason you came all this way to Fort William was to get the fucking number of a train? Carlton, you really do need to get a life.'

'It's not a train, that's the thing it pulls. It's the engine I take the number of. Mostly steam engines and I always wanted to get the one that goes to Kyle of Lochalsh.' They both continued laughing, this time hysterically. The sea was now climbing up over their bodies. Owen lifted the bottle towards his lips for one last time.

'Let's have one final toast, my friend. To Carlton Moss, my new mate. May we remain, friends, until death do us part.' And then the sea finally claimed the earth back and all was silent.

<u>Friendship</u>

They say when the storm blows in then hearts become heavy with the drift
Only then can a bond be made to join the flow,
refusing to be cast aside like driftwood,
circling your life as the current pulls you downstream.
I have heard it said that the North wind gales can cast a shadow that encases the soul in an icy grip.
Only then can a hand reach out to touch you from the depths,
refusing to let you float alone towards the rage.
I have always known that true friendship rides out the storm,
seeking dry land despite the pull.
How many real friends do we meet in one life,
accepting each other for what we are?
How many will we truly stand beside to meet the tempest?

Jo-Jo

No one was really sure why it was called Daisy Lane Farm. I mean it did stand on a winding road that skirted around Loch Arkaig to finish at the big farmhouse of Monadh Lorn, but the track had always been known as the Glendessary road, nothing to do with Daisies or lanes. The name seemed to conjure up images of a quaint Southern English village bathed in flowers rather than a small farm nestled beside a windswept loch in the Scottish Highlands. And yet despite its remote location Daisy Lane Farm was once a happy bustling family home protected from the wind by the tall trees that surrounded it.

When we look back it always feels as though the 1950s had something that both the previous and the proceeding decades could not compete with. The country was beginning to escape from the austerity of war but had yet to embrace the consumer culture and decadence that the future would bring. Maybe they could be called innocent times and for the Fascione family, they were indeed happy and seemingly carefree. And yet we know that this book does not tell a happy tale, how could it? The clouds of despair and gloom were already gathering, but for now, we join the family in the very last golden hours before dark despair completely descended on their hearts.

James and Marie waited patiently on the wall at the junction of the track to Glendessary and the main road. The bus from Moy primary school would drop young Andrew off a good ten to fifteen minutes after the one from the senior school. The two elder siblings had always been incredibly close despite the difference of a year between them. But closeness did not mean similarity. Maybe that was why they bonded so well; their personalities were polar opposites. At 13 Marie was outgoing, chatty, and seemed to be happy-go-lucky. Even at that awkward age, she was starting to grow into her looks. Her dark hair was wild and windswept, her blue eyes would flash with life as she lifted her head in readiness for anything that the boys could throw at her. Already she was becoming the target of desire for the adolescents of the local school.

But even Marie knew that she could not compete with James, or Jo-Jo as everyone knew him. When it came to looks and charisma, he already had it all. At 14 he only had the potential to grow out of his looks rather than into them. Jo-Jo was tall and well-built even for that relatively young age. For the 1950s his deep black hair was unfashionably long at the fringe and would constantly fall over his face. His dark skin would accentuate the deep green eyes that seemed to hint at some inner sadness or turmoil. Jo-Jo was a boy of few words, so much so that when he did speak everyone would hang on his every syllable. The girls loved him for his air of mystery, the boys admired him because he was brave enough to stick up for himself no matter the adversary, and of course, his family adored him because he was Jo-Jo.

The 1934 Leyland Lion school bus was a relic of the past even for the mid-1950s. Jo-Jo and Marie watched it cough and splutter its way up the hill from Lochie. Black exhaust fumes belched out of the back as it struggled to make the ascent to the junction with the Glendessary road. It finally pulled up beside the children with a squeal of worn brakes and the smell of dust and fumes. Jo-Jo jumped off the wall and took a few steps towards the open door just as a little bundle of pent-up ginger excitement leapt from the stairs towards him.

Andrew Fascione was so unlike his older brother in both temperament and looks that the family would often joke that they had picked the wrong baby up from Inverness hospital 9 years previously. For his age, he was small and skinny. His bright orange hair made him the target of fun, but his boundless energy and enthusiasm endeared those who got to know him. 'You promise we are still going hunting tomorrow, Jo-Jo.' His older brother winked at Marie as he peeled the youngster away from his shoulders.

'Of course, he is taking you hunting you dafty. When does Jo-Jo ever say no to his wee brother?'

Marie picked up the school bag her younger sibling had casually dropped on the ground as he leapt into the arms of the older boy. The children continued to walk down the track towards Daisy Lane Farm as the bus started the descent long towards its final destination at Fort Augustus. It would disgorge the last children there before spluttering and clanking to its long-awaited weekend rest at the local depot.

Jo-Jo and Maire said little as they watched the excitable Andy race away in front of them. They kept close to the stone wall that bordered the path as a sharp wind cut across the floor of the glen. Andy had come to an abrupt halt 50 yards in front of them. For once he was not running around and seemed to be lost in thought. As they edged nearer, he raised his head and spoke. 'Why does Uncle Cameron hate dad so much?'

'Andy, you know that God does not like you using words like hate. Uncle Cameron and dad just don't get on. A lot of brothers are like that.' Marie glanced at Jo-Jo as she spoke the words. He remained silent as though the discussion was nothing to do with him.

'Well Jo-Jo is my brother and we get on brilliantly.' With that, the young boy skipped away as though he had already forgotten the conversation. Marie stopped walking and continued to look at the silent Jo-Jo.

'Do you know mum was crying again last night?' Jo-Jo turned to his sister. Their eyes met and finally, he spoke.

'Why?'

'Jo-Jo, you bloody well know why. It's him, that old bastard up the hill, Cameron. He won't let it go. Dad says he is certain that we will get notice to leave the farm soon.' Her brother had sadness in his eyes as he looked away.

'I know, I know, but there is nothing we can do, Mar. Anyway, dad's just as bloody stubborn as he is.' He walked on after his younger brother. Marie followed with her head bowed. They could see the smoke rising from the chimney of Daisy Lane Farm ahead. The back of the house nestled into the trees at the side of the glen while the front faced out into the calm blue water of Loch Arkaig. The girl surveyed the scene with a heavy heart. This had always been home, a happy place that at one time had seemed so stable and forever. A few miles further on up the Glendessary road was the cause of all their problems. The large crumbling farm of Monadh Lorn and its slowly disintegrating occupier. The man with hate in his heart. The one person who could ruin everything for them.

* * *

Alice Fascione stood over the stove; pots simmered on the large range as she busied herself preparing the main meal of the day. She was still a striking-looking woman, even for someone who had delivered three children and spent the first 15 years of her marriage working night and day on the farm. Of course, father time had taken its toll and she looked all of her 35 years but even with her hair tied up and an apron around her waist she was still considered to be the bonniest catch in the glen.

Marie stood beside her mother trying to busy herself although, in reality, she was getting in the way. The similarity in looks between the two women was obvious. The main difference was the worry lines that crossed Alice's brow and crinkled under her blue eyes. The two boys had disappeared out into the hills to find their father. The same ritual would be followed each day as soon as the children arrived back from school. Jo-Jo and Andy were expected to help with the farm chores while Marie would work with her mother to help prepare the main meal of the day.

The kitchen was the largest room in the building, the hub of the Fascione family life. A big wooden table stood in the centre of the floor while all around it the paraphernalia of a busy working farm and a happy family home dominated the scene. Wellington boots, Numerous wooden kitchen utensils, glass jars, baskets of flowers picked from the glen, bowls of water and food for the dogs, coats hanging on racks, everywhere a clutter of a busy working life. And opposite the cooker stood the real heart of the room. A large fireplace that burned constantly. The smell of peat smoke mingled with the various aromas of the evening meal being cooked.

The women had said little to each other as they busied themselves before the men came home. Both knew that words had to come but neither wanted to broach the subject. Marie finally spoke, it was now or never as time was running out and her father would soon be back with the boys. 'Mum, are you ok?' Alice stopped washing the pot that she held in her hands at the large sink. She sighed and waited a few seconds before replying.

'Mar, I've told you before my love, I'm fine. It's just, well you know.' She turned to look at her daughter and smiled before affectionately placing a hand on her forehead and pushing the curls back that had fallen over Marie's eyes. 'You really are so pretty. One day you will find a husband who is as good as your father.' She knew her mother was trying to deflect her from the main subject.

'Mum, what are we going to do? Can dad not just go and try and make up with Uncle Cameron? I know they don't get on and that he hates us but surely he would be ok if dad at least tried to speak to him.' Alice turned back to the sink. Her demeanour made it obvious to her daughter that the conversation was over.

'Mar, I've told you before. Your dad and Cameron won't speak again. It's not your father's fault, he has tried everything but it's no good. If his brother wants us out of the farm, then there is nothing else we can do to change his mind. This goes back a long way and some things just can't be mended.'

The two women continued working in silence while they listened for the bark of the dogs and the clatter of feet to signal that the men were returning home. Alice thought about what Marie had said. She could not be angry with her daughter, 13-year olds saw things in an uncomplicated light. Adults had years of family feuding, bitterness and pride to take into consideration. The long protracted falling out between her husband Leslie and his older brother Cameron went back to their childhood days. Her father-in-law Caseareo Fascione had not been an easy man to get along with. He held the two brothers under his control while running the large family farm of Monadh Lorn. The real problem started when he allowed Leslie to rent the smaller farm at Daisy lane after he married Alice. But that had only been the final nail in the coffin of the two brother's relationship. Everybody including Marie and Jo-Jo knew what the real issue was. It was her, Alice. She had chosen Leslie when all in the glen had expected her to wed Cameron. They had even courted for some months until she backed off. Alice had always been in love with the younger brother, Cameron knew that, but he had expected to be able to pull rank. That was the way it was in the glen. And now he rotted away in a haze of alcohol and bitterness as the head of Monadh Lorn following the passing of his father, Caseareo.

Leslie placed his arms around Alice's waist and looked

over her shoulder at the stew simmering away on the stove. The children sat at the table, Marie talked while Andy bobbed up and down on his chair, his ginger curls flapping around his head. Beside him sat Col, the only one of the four working dogs they had that was given special treatment. The border collie had a bad limp and was no longer any good for helping Leslie on the farm. In normal circumstances, it would have been put down, but Col was Andy's best friend. It followed him everywhere he went and now the family accepted the dog as part of them. As usual, Jo-Jo sat silently smiling and watching the scene around him. The children were used to their father showing affection towards their mother. Leslie could lay down the law with the kids when he needed to, but his quiet easy-going nature endeared him to most who knew him. The children respected their father rather than feared him. And yet despite this being a Friday and the day before the weekend, there was no doubting that the family ate in an unusually subdued atmosphere. Leslie tried to lighten things by tormenting young Andy and ribbing Marie about a boy she liked at school, but the meal still ended as though a shadow hung over the normally happy Farmhouse.

It was nearly 10 o'clock when Alice was finally able to bring the subject up once more. The children had drifted off to their rooms and the couple sat beside the fire with a mug of tea in their hands. Neither drank alcohol even though it was the weekend. Leslie had been tea-total all his life and Alice had followed suit once they were married. The fact that his father had been an alcoholic and that his brother was following the same path was enough for him to abstain.

The ticking of the clock on the mantlepiece was the only noise that broke the silence until Alice spoke. She leaned forward and placed an affectionate hand on her husband's knee. He took a puff from the pipe that dangled from his lips and their eyes met. 'Leslie, my love. I've been thinking about something, something that might help. A last try.' Leslie placed the pipe onto the edge of the ashtray. He knew he did not want to hear the words; the shame was too much for someone who was so proud of his family. He waited until her lips moved once more, the words spoken softly as though the children or even the spirits might hear. 'The letter of notice, we have only a week. Look, my dear. I know you've tried, and he won't listen, How about…' Her husband sat back abruptly and spoke with unusual sharpness.

'Alice, no. I won't have you going near that place. He is a drunkard and totally unreasonable. He listens to no one except his own black heart. It would be pointless and he's dangerous. You know that he turned the shotgun on me the last time I tried to speak to him. We will leave, unless a miracle happens, we will pack and go. Cousin Hugh in Inverness will help us until I can find work.' He stopped talking as tears started to run down his beloved wife's face.

Cameron stood up before placing his arms around her. She remained seated and looked up at him.

'Leslie, you've only ever known Daisy Lane and Monadh Lorn, it's in your blood to farm. What else are we going to do to earn money to live and how do we look after the children?' She was crying now but suddenly her tears turned to anger. 'What right does that bastard have to throw us out of our own home?' He hugged his wife close before replying.

'He has every right. He inherited the farms and the land. Have you told the children yet that we leave next weekend?' By the silence that followed he knew she had yet to bring up the subject. Of course, the children understood the situation but not the gravity of them only having a week left. But this time Leslie was reading her response wrong. Alice was not thinking about the children, it was the man on the hill who was clouding her thoughts. She would go to Monadh Lorn tomorrow and do whatever it took to get Cameron to change his mind.

Upstairs the children were going through their usual routine in an attempt to try and get Andy to go to sleep or at least leave the two older siblings to talk in peace. Jo-Jo play wrestled with him and then read another chapter from Treasure Island. The youngster hung on every word his big brother spoke as he added his own drama into the tale. Eventually, Andy settled down after Marie threatened to lock his beloved dog Col outside if he did not go to sleep.

Marie and Jo-Jo wandered off to their rooms leaving Andy and his border collie companion nestled together in the bed.

The upper floor of the farm had been a 1920s conversion of the attic. The building being large enough to support five bedrooms. At times in the past the family had let out spare rooms for extra income but now very few visitors came to the glen and the youngsters had the run of the upstairs floor.

Unusually Marie followed her older brother into his room rather than her own. They both sat down on the edge of his bed. He had expected this, they had to talk no matter how much he tried to avoid the problem once more. 'Jo-Jo, you do know that mum and dad have been given notice to leave the farm. I think it's next weekend.' This news took her brother by surprise. His usual calmness evaporated for a few seconds before he composed himself and lowered his gaze down to the floor again.

'Nah, don't be daft Mar. Dad would have told me. I know we're getting thrown out but even that bastard Cameron wouldn't do it that soon.' Marie shook her head with impatience. She was becoming so frustrated with being the only one of the three children who seemed to understand the gravity of the situation. She replied to him with a sharpness in her voice.

'For heaven's sake Jo-Jo. You can't bury your head in the sand all your life. Sometimes you need to do something.'

'How do you know it might be next weekend?' Marie

tried to calm down and placed her hand on his arm as she responded.

'I heard them talking last night. As soon as we come upstairs it's all they go on about. That's why mum is always crying. Jo-Jo, do you not notice anything? You could tell tonight at the table. Mum was about to burst into tears and dad was not his usual self either. He hasn't been for months.'

This time Jo-Jo did look up and stare into her eyes as he spoke. 'It will be ok, Mar. I promise it will all work out.' She said nothing. There were no words left to say. Somehow, she knew that Jo-Jo would do whatever he could. That was his way. He had always come good in the past and looked after her and wee Andy. He would do it again, it was the only hope she had left now.

* * *

Saturday morning dawned as the grey sky sent wind-tossed rain down onto the glen below. Jo-Jo had to finally admit to himself that things were not right with his father. He walked into the kitchen at 7 a.m. to find his mother sitting at the table with a mug of tea. 'Where's dad, he usually wakes me if I sleep in?'

'Your father has already gone to Lochie for supplies. He said to leave you be this morning.' They both knew that this was nonsense. Leslie required, even demanded that his oldest son helped him with the farm at the weekend. Jo-Jo accepted his role and fully expected to take over Daisy Lane once his father could no longer manage it.

'What, dad's gone away into town in the motor without me?'

The 1940s land rover was Leslie's pride and joy. He had never been a man for frivolity and luxury, and he would never admit that the car meant anything to him, but the family knew. They could tell by the look of pride on his face each time he started the engine. He would clean it each Sunday without fail. The metal gleamed in the sun as he polished every square inch. His father Caseareo had purchased it new in Inverness for £450. When he passed away it had been the only thing that Cameron had given him other than permission to remain on Daisy Lane Farm rent-free. Leslie knew his brother grudged handing over the land rover even though he had got to keep Monadh Lorn, the Bentley, and all the farm machinery. What stuck in Leslie's throat, even more, was that Cameron left the tractors and other equipment to rot while he drank away his father's money. Eventually, Leslie convinced Alice to agree to pay £120 for the land rover rather than take it for nothing. It was almost their whole life savings. Cameron had looked at his brother as though he was dirt on his shoe as he took the money and slammed the door in his face without saying a word. It had probably been the penultimate act in their disintegrating relationship. And now a few years later, the final scene was being played out as the elder sibling demanded Daisy lane Farm back.

'Can you check the hens for me and do the rest of the chores this morning Jo-Jo? I need to go out. Get Marie and Andy to help you. Your father will be back at noon and will no doubt want you out on the hills with him.' Alice stood up and pulled her woollen coat around her shoulders. She wore a faded flower-patterned dress and even though she had wellington boots on, and her hair tied up she still looked young and vibrant. It was her eyes that gave away the sadness. Dark rings had appeared under them and her usual zest for life seemed to be dimmed.

'Where are you going mum, it's pouring down outside?' She was already half out of the door before she replied.

'I, I need to go on an errand. I'll take the bicycle. I'll be fine Jo-Jo, just do as I ask.'

Alice closed the door hastily behind her as the dogs barked and tried to follow outside. Jo-Jo walked to the kitchen window and pulled back the curtain. His mother was wheeling the bike up towards the Glendessary Road. He watched her jump on as the rain lashed down. She turned left and cycled away with her head down. That way the track only went to one destination, Monadh Lorn Farm. Jo-Jo waited for a few minutes before grabbing his coat and throwing on his boots. His mother had taken the only decent bicycle, there was only one way he would be able to catch her up without transport. He would have to cut through Arkaig forest to miss out on the bend in the track. Alice would have 3 miles to go, it would only be 2 for him, but hard going in this rain. Without a word to his siblings, he was off and running along the edge of the Loch, his boots squelching in the mud and water, his head down to fend off the driving rain and wind.

Jo-Jo kept out of sight behind the dry-stone wall that surrounded the old imposing main building of Monadh Lorn Farm. He crouched down leaving just his head peering over the top towards the entrance. The wind was whipping down the glen causing the rain to constantly change direction, dark clouds swirled in anger over the brow of the imposing hills. He found it hard to believe that this was the same place he remembered as a young child when his Grandfather owned it. In those days it had been a proud working farm, well looked after and able to pay its way. Now the building looked forlorn and sad, no longer cared for by human hands. Slowly decaying just like the man locked inside.

He could see his mother propping the bike against the main gate and then walking with her head bowed in the wind as she made her way to the main entrance. Jo-Jo felt as though he should jump out and shout to her to stop but something held him back. He had not been up this way for years; the last time was with his father when they had been chased off by his crazy uncle wielding an old shotgun.

He watched as his mother banged on the large oak door. Jo-Jo was praying that there would be no answer and she would instead leave and head back home. It felt as if time stood still in those few minutes while she repeatedly rapped the large wooden frame and pressed the bell. Suddenly he could just make out her head moving forward as if she was speaking to someone although in the rain he could not see if the door had been opened. And then she was gone, almost as though the house had swallowed her up inside. Jo-Jo felt as though he was trapped in no man's land. A sense of fear and dread overwhelmed him, but he knew he could neither go after his mother nor leave her alone in this dreadful place. Ten minutes passed as the rain soaked into his body before he crept forward towards the building. He had no intention of making his presence known but he felt compelled to at least get closer and see if he could hear or see anything.

Jo-Jo stood with his back to the side wall of the main house. He was close to what looked like the kitchen window. The glass was smashed, and the hole had been covered with cardboard and old newspapers. Opposite him stood various run-down outbuildings and sheds. The whole place seemed to reek of desolation and abandonment. He could hear the sound of what seemed like raised voices coming through the window. It was impossible to make out what was being said through the noise of the wind and rain. A dog was also barking loudly inside one of the outbuildings.

Suddenly Jo-Jo heard a scream followed by a loud crack. He started to run around to the front door, no longer scared now that his mother was in danger. But he had hardly moved a few steps when the Alsatian was upon him. A mass of snarling teeth and dripping saliva. It sank its jaws into his arm and would not let go despite his desperate attempts to break free. Jo-Jo looked around frantically searching for a means of escape. The dog was dragging him along back towards the outbuilding. He could see blood running down his arm, but adrenalin and the sheer will to survive drowned out the pain. He lost his footing in the wet mud and tumbled over onto the ground. His free hand touched something solid and his fingers grasped it. Incredibly the dog remained latched onto his arm, its white teeth glistening in the rain. Jo-Jo tried to regain his feet but now he had something to even up the contest. He brought the brick crashing down onto the dog's head. It let go of him immediately and ran off towards one of the huts whimpering in pain. The injured boy crawled back to the wall of the building, a trail of blood following him. He could just make out the figure of his mother walking back to the bike she had left only thirty minutes previously.

***

Alice continued to wrap the bandage around her son's arm as he sat silently beside the large kitchen table. She was ashen-faced, and her hands were shaking with shock while she busied herself trying to help her boy. Alice studied Jo-Jo's face but as usual, he gave few clues away. 'I still think when your father gets back, he should run you into Inverness, you might need a few stitches in that.' She spoke the words as though they were a question rather than a statement. Alice knew he was lying. Wild dogs did not just appear out on the hills. They had to belong somewhere. Her face was close to his as she pinned the bandage into place.

'I'll be fine mum. It's just a graze, don't worry about it.' Alice looked directly at him as she replied. He could already sense that she was close to crying.

'Jo-Jo, Look at me. Just look at me for a second' He turned his gaze from the floor and looked up.

'Please Jo-Jo. Don't tell your father that I went to Monadh Lorn. I beg you Jo-Jo, it will kill him if he knew I had gone against his wishes.' Her son continued to look at her and took a few seconds to respond. It was as though he knew what had happened and was afraid to hear anymore.

'Mum, what did he say? Cameron, what did he say, what did he do?' She looked away now, tears rolling down her cheeks.

'Nothing son, he did nothing. He is an old drunk who will listen to no one. He wasn't interested in anything I had to say.' Jo-Jo did not believe her, and he now knew that only he could solve this.

'Mum, I won't say anything to dad. He won't see the bandage; I'll keep my big woollen jumper over it until it heals.' Alice patted her son's arm and then bent down and kissed his forehead.

'I know you want to fix all this Jo-Jo; you always do. But trust me, son, there is nothing to fix anymore. This will all work out; I just have a feeling it will. Your father has made up his mind but maybe things might change. Just let it all play out.' Jo-Jo was not taking in his mother's words anymore. His eyes looked to the ground; his mind was made up. Suddenly Alice put her hands on his face and lifted his gaze towards her. 'Jo-Jo, are you listening to me?' There was a sharpness in her voice now, almost hysterical. 'Look at me Jo-Jo. Tell me you will let things be. Promise me you will not go back to Monadh Lorn, promise me now.' He stared at his mother for a few seconds, his deep eyes lost in another world.

'Yes, I promise mum. I won't go back.' She remained holding her son's face for a few seconds longer.

'Promise me Jo-Jo. You are only fourteen, it's not your responsibility to fix this.' He looked away again before replying once more.

'I won't go to Monadh Lorn, I won't go anywhere near Uncle Cameron.' Alice nodded her head but inside she was still not convinced. She knew her son took after her husband

and his brother when it came to being stubborn.

That evening after an unusually sombre Saturday family dinner Leslie said he had something to tell the children. The three youngsters remained seated at the kitchen table as their father spoke. Even Andy realised the gravity of the situation and for once he kept still and listened. Col stayed at his feet but was hidden under the table. Leslie explained that they would need to be out of the farm by this time next weekend. He had already been into Lochie to organise help from friends. Big Tam and Dave had offered their truck to move their meagre belongings as most of the furniture belonged to the farm. They would be staying with Cousin Hugh in Inverness until he could find somewhere permanent for them. An ashen-faced Marie asked how they would get to school but Leslie explained that events had happened so fast that he still had to work the details out. Both he and Alice would be driving to Inverness tomorrow to get things agreed upon.

The children had expected their father to give them his usual list of chores and instructions to do while he was away. This time he took them by surprise by simply saying, 'Just enjoy the day tomorrow. If the rain stays off why don't the three of you go out into the hills? I promise you, my loves, one day we will come back.' For a moment it looked as though the usually controlled Leslie was about to break. Instead, he turned to Alice and pulled her towards him before kissing her. Strangely their mother said nothing, she seemed to be lost in her own thoughts.

The youngsters asked no further questions, they knew the decision had been made and any further discussion would be futile. In reality, the children, even young Andy to a degree had known this was coming. Their parents had tried to convince themselves that they were hiding the grim situation from the kids at least until all hope was gone. It was all a charade, all in the family knew the truth. Their father and his brother Cameron had always been on a collision course that would inevitably end in the loss of Daisy Lane Farm.

* * *

Marie sat on the stool beside the dressing table in her night dress. She stared into the mirror and combed her long dark hair while mulling over the day's events. A growing sense of resignation and finality was creeping over her. There seemed no way out of the horrible situation that had beset the family. Even Jo-Jo could not change the way the cards were being dealt. *Maybe Inverness will be good for us all. A clean break away from the shadow of Monadh Lorn.* She repeated the words in her head without any real conviction. The Fascione's were not city people, they belonged in the hills. They belonged here, at Daisy lane farm.

There was a tap on the bedroom door and a few seconds

later Jo-Jo walked in. She felt like scolding him for invading her privacy without waiting to be asked but said nothing. He sat down on the edge of her bed and remained silent. That was the way with Jo-Jo, even if he had something to say, you still needed to ask questions to get it out of him.

'Is Andy asleep?'

'I doubt it. Wee rascal is pretending he is. He was quiet tonight though; poor wee soul is scared about the move.' Marie turned to look at her brother. She knew he had not come into her room to talk about Andy.

'What is it Jo-Jo? Tell me what you're thinking.' He took her by surprise by answering quickly. For once the words were not spoken in his usual soft calm tone. His voice sounded hard, almost as though the adult Jo-Jo had taken over the child before its time.

'We have to sort this out Mar. I need you to come with me tomorrow when mum and dad are in Inverness.' She did not have to ask where they were going. It was what they were going to do that scared her.

'What can we do Jo-Jo? It was up to mum and dad to sort this out, I can't see how us talking to Cameron can help.' Suddenly Jo-Jo stood up and walked over to his sister. He took her by the shoulders and looked deep into her eyes. She had rarely known her brother to look directly at her, most of the time he spoke with his gaze fixed on the ground.

'Listen Mar. Mum went to see that old bastard this

morning.' His voice started to crack as he spoke. 'Something happened, he did something to mum. I don't know what it was, but she was really upset when she returned.' Marie had tears in her eyes now.

'What, what shall we do Jo-Jo?' He shook his head. The Man boy was in control now. He had made his decision and would not go back on it. She understood that and would also do what was required.

'We need to go to Monadh Lorn. See Cameron, convince him to change his mind.'

'But Jo-Jo, what's the point if he won't listen? How is it going to be any different if he wouldn't listen to mum? You know as well as I do that, he still loves her. That's why he hates dad and us as well.' Marie knew the answer, even though she dreaded being told what the solution would have to be.

'We break in and find his gun, the one he chased me and dad with a few years back. There is nothing else we can do. We shoot the bastard and make it look like he committed suicide. Who is really going to be surprised? He is a bloody miserable old alcoholic, sitting up there rotting on the farm he got from Grandad. It should have gone to dad not him. Why the hell did Grandad not leave a will, he must have known that Cameron would make a mess of things.' Marie continued to listen to her brother, a mixture of fear and hope in her eyes.

'Jo-Jo, people are not daft. Even if we could do what you say, the police, everyone knows that dad would get the farm if something happened to Cameron. They would be suspicious right away.' He turned from her and started to walk towards the door before stopping, his head once again looking down. The little lost boy was back.

'I don't care Mar, what does it matter now? I'll take the blame if they find out. It's me who needs to do what has to be done. You can stay outside; I just need someone else as a lookout while I go into the house.' She sighed before replying.

'Of course, I'll help Jo-Jo. You're right, we've no choice. We need to do this for mum and dad.'

Jo-Jo opened the door and walked back to his room. In the shadow of the unlit upstairs hallway, he did not see the young boy hiding on the other side of his sister's room. Andy had placed his ear to the door and heard everything that had been said.

* * *

Sunday dawned over Daisy Lane Farm as though the weather knew that the final act was about to be played out. Angry black clouds fought against each other to keep the sun hidden as if they were trying to stop it from getting involved. And yet between the squally showers that shifted constantly on the wind an occasional ray of sunshine would break through. At that moment peace would descend on the little farm as if it was frozen in time, almost like a still photograph capturing the faded happiness of children playing and a young couple very much in love.

Marie watched from the window of the kitchen as the land rover rattled over the stones and mud of the courtyard and out onto the Glendessary road. At that very moment, the sun shone down on the car just for a few fleeting seconds before the dark clouds once more gained the upper hand. She knew it would be the last flicker of light before her parents would be plunged into recrimination and regret. There was no going back now. Marie turned towards the stairs as she heard the footsteps of her brother coming down from his room. She expected to see Jo-Jo but was taken aback when first of all Col came limping through the door followed by Andy. Behind him came her elder sibling, his face pale and angry.

'What's happening, I thought we agreed that Andy was to stay in his room until we get back?' It was not Jo-Jo who answered, it was her younger brother.

'You're not going to shoot Uncle Cameron without me. I want to come too.' Marie looked in shock before addressing the older boy who stood framed in the doorway.

'Bloody hell Jo-Jo, what are we going to do now.' He did not answer, his actions told her all that she needed to know. Jo-Jo grabbed his boots and sat down at the table to put them on. He then stood up and walked over to the cabinet at the back of the kitchen before taking out his father's shotgun. He carefully counted out the cartridges and placed them into his pocket. Marie took Andy's jacket from the rack and made him put it on. 'Get your coat on Andy and we're not taking that bloody old dog with us.'

'Yes, we are Mar, Col will look after us. He needs to come too. Please Mar, please.'

'Andy, this is not some daft game we're going to play. Jo-Jo, tell him.' Marie looked to her older sibling for support, but he was already walking towards the door, the gun slung over his shoulder.

'Bring the bloody dog with you. What does it matter, we need to get this done and now.' He pulled the handle and stepped out into the wind and rain. Marie, Andy, and Col scrambled after him into the morning gloom.

This time Jo-Jo followed the Glendessary road to Monadh Lorn rather than the shorter route through the forest. They could just make out the blue water of Loch Arkaig shimmering on the left through the trees. In happier times the children had swam in the water and played amongst the tall pines. Nothing could have been further from the minds of the three siblings as they trudged in silence towards the head of the glen and their uncle's run-down farm. Only young Andy did not fully comprehend the seriousness of what was about to unfold. Maybe he was aware of the danger ahead but to him, it all still felt like a game. Bringing up the rear of the strange little group came Col, limping and sniffing the ground as he struggled to keep up. The older children said nothing, words were no longer required. It was a time for action rather than talk.

It took more than an hour in the rough weather to reach the rusting gates of Monadh Lorn farm. As they stood huddled together looking at the imposing building the clouds seemed to part allowing the sun to grab its chance. To Marie, it felt surreal that the weather would suddenly brighten up at the very point they were about to commit the darkest of deeds. She looked at the still figure of their leader and waited for him to speak. His face looked down and for a few minutes, Marie hoped that he had changed his mind. He finally lifted his head and gave her a sad smile. His green eyes still looked youthful despite the dark circles underneath. The wild fringe of his hair brushed over his face with the wind.

'You two wait here. I'll go on my own to do this. Keep hidden on the other side of the gate and if you hear anyone coming up the road then you need to come and get me.' Marie stepped forward and put her hand on his shoulder.

'No, Jo-Jo, this needs to be the two of us. Andy can keep a lookout.' She expected him to protest and was surprised when he took the gun from his shoulder and carefully loaded it before handing it to Andy. The young boy's eyes widened with the knowledge that his beloved older brother was trusting him with such a responsible task. Marie was puzzled. 'Surely we need the gun if we're going to do what you said?' Jo-Jo replied with sad resignation breaking over his voice.

'Don't be daft Mar. We need Uncle Cameron's gun if we are going to make it look like he shot himself.' It was beginning to dawn on her that Jo-Jo had as always thought things through. Suddenly she could see light at the end of the tunnel. *Maybe this will all work out after all.* Jo-Jo turned towards the farmhouse. 'Come on, Mar, let's go.' But before he moved off, he spoke sternly to young Andy. 'Keep the gun pointed at the ground and stay here. Only go into the farm if you hear me shout or because someone is coming up the track.' Andy smiled and nodded his head.

'Ok, Jo-Jo, I will, I promise.' Jo-Jo walked over to him and knelt down.

'Andy, listen to me. This is not a game, do you understand?'

'Yes' Jo-Jo, I know. We're here to kill Uncle Cameron because he hates dad and loves mum and wants our farm.' The elder boy stood up and looked over at Marie. They both smiled sadly and walked off towards the house.

Within a few minutes, they had edged up to the front door. Jo-Jo had warned his sister to keep silent in case the dog that had attacked him was still around. The light wind rustling in the trees was giving them cover for now at least. He tried the door handle half expecting it to be unlocked and was dismayed to find it bolted. 'Shit, we'll have to try around the back. We need to go the other way though, passed the big windows at the front. We can't risk going near the sheds in case that bloody Alsatian is still here.' Marie nodded her head and followed him. A few hundred yards away at the gate, Andy stood and watched. The gun pointed firmly down at his feet, Col sitting obediently at his side.

They crawled under the main windows of the house in case their uncle was in one of the lower rooms and finally reached the back of the building. The once proud farm was even more derelict from the rear. Discarded household rubbish and broken machinery littered the muddy courtyard. Jo-Jo stepped carefully over the empty whisky and beer bottles that had been dumped just outside the rear entrance. This time there was no need to try the handle, the door was already half open. He tried to push it to gain entrance only to recoil in horror at the sound of crashing bottles. Both of them stood still and said nothing for what seemed like an age. No sound came from inside and eventually, Jo-Jo managed to squeeze through the opening by stepping over the pile of used containers.

Once inside the two children stood nervously together in the gloom. Even though the sun still shone outside it was difficult to see clearly as the windows were either covered by torn curtains or worse by a thick green grime. The hallway was littered with rubbish and dog excrement. Jo-Jo signalled to Marie to wait while he searched the lower rooms. She stood in the hallway for the next ten minutes terrified that her uncle or even worse one of his dogs would appear. Finally, she heard Jo-Jo coming back. He looked dejected. 'I found the gun cabinet; I knew where it was as I remember when we used to come up here years ago. When dad and Cameron still spoke. It's empty, every bloody gun is gone.'

'What are we going to do Jo-Jo? Maybe we should just leave this and get out of here.' She spoke the words in a frightened pleading tone hoping he would feel the same.

'No, I'm going upstairs. We came here to do this, even if I have to kill the old bastard with my bare hands.'

'Jo-Jo, please, this is crazy. You said we were going to make it look like suicide. How the hell can we do that without his gun.' Her words had fallen on deaf ears as he was already carefully dodging the bottles and junk to climb the stairs. Marie eventually followed and soon the two children stood on the landing next to the closed door of what they knew to be their uncle's bedroom.

'I need to go in alone Mar. You stay here. If it goes wrong for me then you have to run, get Andy and get the hell out of this place.' He placed his hand on her arm and even though it was difficult to see, she knew he was looking at her. This was it. The end game had arrived. Marie took his hand from her shoulder and squeezed it.

'Please be careful Jo-Jo, we love you. I need you and Andy needs you. Please come back.' He edged up to the door and again found it obstructed by what seemed like bottles and junk on the other side. This time he put his shoulder to the frame and abandoned any pretence of keeping quiet. The door burst open to the sound of splintering glass as he crunched over the rubbish and walked in. It was the stench that hit him first. The room was pitch black and the smell was almost unbearable. Jo-Jo felt his way to the window and tore down the heavy curtains that kept out the daylight.

In the hallway, Marie stood transfixed in the gloom as she listened to the commotion coming from her uncle's bedroom. She recoiled in horror as her brother seemed to lose all abandon as he crashed around the room. And then suddenly all went quiet. The world stopped turning for those few moments of utter silence as she waited in despair for the outcome of this madness. But it was the last thing she expected to hear that would etch the moment in her memory for the rest of her life. It started with Jo-Jo chuckling and then it built up into a laugh, a manic laugh as though he had finally gone over the edge. She burst into the room and was shocked to see the sunlight flooding in. Her eyes took a few seconds to adjust and then the smell hit her. Marie stood transfixed as she was finally able to take in the macabre scene. Jo-Jo was kneeling beside the bed still laughing hysterically.

What looked like the torso of her Uncle Cameron lay half out of the bed covers. Most of his head was missing, and dried-out red blotches and pieces of bone were splattered over the wall behind him. The gun lay over his legs along with more bottles. Some of them still contained liquid. The young girl tried her best to block out the awful vision and stepped over to her brother. 'What, what the hell happened Jo-Jo, what did you do?' He finally stopped laughing and looked up at her. His face was white with shock, and his eyes sunk deep into the dark rings that surrounded them.

'I didn't do anything Mar. That's what's so funny. We never needed to do anything, that's why mum was warning me not to come here.'

'What do you mean Jo-Jo, what are you talking about?' He started to chuckle again, the sound of a young boy who could no longer face growing into a man if this is what it all meant.

'Can you not see Mar. Look, look at him. It's mum. He never did anything to her yesterday when she came here. It was mum who did it, she beat us to it.' And then he laughed again, each guffaw sounding more insane than the last.

Andy watched the front door of Monadh Lorn intently. More than thirty minutes had passed, and he was starting to feel scared. The game had suddenly become too real. It wasn't that he was worried about Jo-Jo and Mar, he trusted his big brother implicitly and knew he would return safe and sound. It was Col, he had started whimpering and was now growling in the direction of the farm. His beloved dog never did this, she was always quiet, obedient and docile. 'Shut up Col, you're scaring me, please stop it.'

It was at the very moment Col really started to bark that he saw Jo-Jo and Mar running out of the front door. Andy was so relieved that he forgot his brother's instruction to stay at the gate and took off towards them. The young boy had hardly taken a few steps when he saw the horror unfolding before his eyes. Neither of his siblings could see the large Alsatian hurtling behind them. Its white teeth bared for the attack, its jaws dripping with saliva. Andy screamed and then stopped in his tracks. Col was flying towards the enemy, his old legs refusing to be held back by the limp. Jo-Jo and Marie stood transfixed as their little brother's treasured companion latched its jaws onto the much bigger dog. Within seconds the mismatch became apparent. The massive beast was ripping into the flesh of the older dog. Jo-Jo made a vain attempt to help Col but was sent flying with the brute force of the battle. Suddenly there was a loud crack followed by a splatter of blood and bones.

Mar stood over Jo-jo and helped him to his feet. They looked in disbelief at the new macabre scene before their eyes. It was hard to comprehend but this was even worse than what they had just witnessed in their uncle's bedroom. Young Andy was standing transfixed as he held the smoking shotgun still pointing at the remains of the two dogs. The blast had blown both of the animals to pieces. All that seemed to be left was the quivering torso of the Alsatian and blobs of white fur that had once been attached to his beloved Companion Col.

***

Marie stood lost in her memories as she stared at the ruin of Daisy Lane Farm. This was as far as she intended to go up the Glendessary track. John her husband was already reversing the car in readiness to return to the main road and go back to their hotel in Fort William. He had always known that she would not go all the way to Monadh Lorn even though she had said she wanted to see it one final time. John knew the story though; he knew that Daisy Lane Farm had been the last time she had really been happy until she met him and had her own children.

50 years had passed by since the Fascione family had moved out of the little farm to take over Monadh Lorn. Marie could pinpoint the exact moment that everything disintegrated even though it was supposed to be the start of their new life. It wasn't the day they had found their uncle's body; it was six months later when the family finally got the keys to Monadh Lorn and their father insisted they move out of Daisy Lane to take control of what was now rightfully his.

John drove the car a few hundred yards down the road to allow Marie some solitude as she climbed over the stones that had once held the gate in place. A light summer wind was rustling through the crumbling ruins of the house. The roof had collapsed long ago, and a lot of the stonework had been removed by the current owners of Monadh Lorn for use elsewhere. And yet the spirit of the little farm remained embedded in the fading remains. She could still feel the happy memories of long ago, the shouts of the children, a youthful-looking Alice staring out of the kitchen window smiling as the youngsters played in the garden. The dogs running and barking as they heralded the return of her father. The rattle of the exhaust as his beloved land rover clattered over the rough stones of the compact courtyard.

Life had become so busy since she left in 1960 to go to college. In reality, Marie had been glad to get away and grab her destiny. Things had never been the same for the family once they inherited Monadh Lorn. Her mother and father seemed to lose that youthful happy spark they had at Daisy Lane. Leslie became engrossed in trying to prove to the locals that he was the opposite of his brother. Work became everything to him, and he drove the boys just as hard in the hope that they would eventually take over the farm together. It didn't work out that way, no matter how much he might have wanted it to.

Marie felt her eyes water as she thought about Jo-Jo.

She had largely managed to put him to the back of her memory over the years in the hope that she would not make the same mistakes with her children. He had become even more introverted after the horror of the day they had gone to Monadh Lorn intending to murder their uncle. When she left for college Jo-jo was already on medication for depression. His deep green eyes no longer sparkled with life. If it was possible, he spoke even less than he had before. Just two years later he was dead. The boy who had planned to take someone's life had finally succeeded in his quest by taking his own.

It was only her and Andy who were left now. Her young brother had easily managed to move on from even the horror of shooting Col. That was the way of children, youth gave them the ability to quickly adjust and look forward rather than back. She smiled at the thought of the red-headed youngster who was now retired with 8 grandchildren and his own farm in Australia. The last time she had met him had been almost 30 years previously when he had come back to Scotland for their mother's funeral. Alice had only been in her mid-fifties when she passed away in 1975. Like Jo-Jo her mother never seemed the same once they left Daisy Lane. There were still some good times, some laughter but somehow a shadow seemed to hang over the Fascione's after Cameron supposedly took his own life. The circumstances of his death were never discussed, not by Jo-Jo and certainly not by Alice.

When her mother died of cancer a decade or so after her son passed away it was as if the family had finally paid their dues and could at long last call Monadh Lorn their own. Of course, by then it was too late. Marie and Andy had moved on to live their own lives while Jo-Jo and Alice had taken their secret to the grave. Only Leslie was left to work the farm while the shadow of his long-dead brother watched over him. Meanwhile further down the valley Daisy Lane slowly crumbled into ruin.

Marie turned around and started to walk back to the car. She still felt remorse and regret for not attending her father's funeral some years back. It was hard for her to admit but somehow maybe she blamed Leslie just as much as Cameron for the death of her brother. It was only at that point that she noticed the heavily overgrown courtyard at the side of the ruin. It reminded her of happier times when she would watch out of the kitchen window as her father and the boys returned from the hills. Now large trees had taken root in the driveway, tall grass was growing around fallen blocks that had once been part of a side wall.

It was something glistening in the sun that caught her eye. Marie edged through the weeds to look. She knew immediately what it was. Her father's much-loved land rover had been abandoned in the drive. It had lain there so long that the body of the car had sunk into the ground and the roof had collapsed onto the seats. It made her smile as she thought about her father. Maybe he had known that one day she would return to Daisy Lane rather than Monadh Lorn and he had left it there so he could finally say goodbye. Could it even have been his way of saying sorry?

Marie finally walked back to her husband who waited in the car. She would not return to Glendessary again. The girl who had first left in 1960 had never really been back since. She had visited occasionally but the heart of the family had already been torn out. Her spirit had long since flown and now her guilt had finally joined it to float away across the shimmering blue water of Loch Arkaig.

Car Graveyard

Metallic, shiny, once loved
King of the B road, once someone's pride, once someone's joy
Rusted, grass-grown, lonely except for its silent decaying friends
No piston roar, no ignition spark, just memories of happy miles tread

Metal, rubber, glass, once polished, once caressed
King of the A road, once someone's friend, once someone's desire
Broken, going, merging back into the earth
No piston roar, no ignition spark
Just a mirror of time, just a bearer of life.

Money Can Buy Me, Love

Hire Car

There are no company logos or writing on the blue Ford Focus to say that it's a hire car but Sherlock Holmes or even a middle-grade detective would be able to tell you that it is. I suppose they would look at the bigger picture and nod with confident arrogance before showing you how clever they are. 'Yes, I can see that this is a hire car simply by considering all the facts.'

'Eh, how the hell can you tell by just looking at the vehicle?'

'Easy, you need to rise above the scene and see the bigger picture.'

'Ok, go on then, enlighten me.'

'Well first of all the obvious. The Ford Focus is used by many UK hire companies as a compact and reasonably cost-effective vehicle for those who want to do short to medium journeys. Secondly, the lady standing beside the car smoking a cigarette is middle-aged, attractive, and tastefully dressed. I get the impression she is going to meet someone. It's the fact that she is thinking about her rendezvous that makes me wonder if this is a secret and that would also point to a hire car. And the third thing, well this is what really gives it all away.

'Ok, yes go on, tell me the key point of your deduction.'

'Well my friend, look at the way she is leaning against the front bonnet taking another inhale of that cigarette, do you see?'

'Yes, yes, I do, but how does that prove it's a hire car?'

'Well stop asking questions for a second and I will tell you. Look at the cigarette ash falling onto the bonnet. Watch how little she cares that by leaning and almost sitting on the paintwork she may well be scratching what is almost a brand-new motor vehicle. This seals the deal for me. She may have tried to look good today, but the woman is not wearing designer shoes or expensive clothes. If that was hers and she had just bought it then she would be wiping fingerprints off the metallic blue paint and staring lovingly at her new toy. Instead, she is flicking ash on it because she does not care. That my friend proves it's a hire car.

And you know what? Our intrepid Inspector Clouseau would be spot on. It's a hire car that has stopped in the layby of the A74 just a few miles short of Beattock Summit in the Scottish Borders. What he wouldn't be able to tell you is that the lady standing smoking and lost in thought is Lorna McGarvey. She looks to be in her late forties, maybe early fifties, slim, around 5 feet 7, long dark hair, and deep thoughtful green eyes. She is dressed tastefully but in jeans and a tight-fitting white top that accentuates her curves. You get the impression that she has tried to look her best even though she can't afford expensive clothes. In fact, this is probably the best outfit she has.

Lorna takes one last puff of her cigarette before flicking it to the ground and stubbing it out with her left foot. It's only then that you notice she is wearing trainers. It just doesn't look right, almost as though getting dressed up for the occasion only reached down to her ankles. Oh, and one final thing to tell you before we begin our tale. Lorna McGarvey now calls herself Georgie and she is indeed on a journey to meet someone. This person holds her entire future in his hands, absolutely everything and yet she has never met him in person. The hired blue Ford Focus will sort that out for her though. For the rest of us, we will need to go back in time to see how Georgie got herself into this situation in the first place.

Domestic Bliss

Charlie McGarvey asked Lorna Swinton to marry him in the spring of 1992. Well, maybe not ask, he probably told her she was getting married. He was 24 and his soon-to-be bride was 5 years younger at 19. They had met at the dancing in Dumfries the year before and had been inseparable ever since. They looked an odd match as she was 5 feet 7 while Charlie or Chick as he was then known came in at a diminutive 5 feet 4. Even in those days, Chick was losing his hair and within a few years he had shaved the remains off. The couple soon settled into supposed domestic bliss at their medium-sized terrace house in Dumfries and one by one the boys arrived. First, there was Adam in 1995, Charlie Junior in 1997, and finally Brendon in 2000. A close and seemingly happy little family who strived to do their best for the boys. Chick toiled away as a salesman for the large local plastics company and eventually moved into sales management and decent money. Lorna or Lori as she was known to those close to her looked after the children and also worked part-time in a small boutique in the town centre.

Now you are probably thinking that this all sounds rather boring; you might even be starting to nod off if you're reading this in your bed. Stick with me because all is not what it may seem. The marriage problems had probably always been there, shuffling around in the background but with three young boys to bring up Lorna just accepted her lot. Chick had been the first man she had really been out with. Maybe there had been a few dates with others, but Lori had always lacked confidence even though she would have been considered pretty by most of her peer group. When she looked back and tried to remember her youth it dawned on her that she had never really loved Chick. In fact, she had never loved anyone, or at least she felt as though she had never experienced true love. So, life just ambled on from one year to the next until eventually, the boys left home one by one. The last to go was Charlie junior in 2019 and the minute he walked out of the door was when Lorna finally admitted to herself that her life was now empty. The three children had been everything to her, the only reason she existed.

'You will need to watch your weight, Lori. Now that you don't have the boys to run around after you will soon lose your figure.' Lorna was standing over the sink washing the dishes while Charlie sat at the kitchen table finishing his evening meal. The comment wasn't deliberately meant to be calculated and cruel. It was just what the couple had become used to. Charlie could say what he wanted because he was the breadwinner, it was he who looked after the money; indeed, it was he who looked after everything. The imbalance had always been there, but it was only now that it started to bite as the empty nest arrived.

I was thinking about joining a gym or maybe even taking up running or cycling now that the boys are away, and I have more time.' Charlie almost choked on the last few chips he had already placed in his mouth.

'You, running or cycling. Don't make me laugh, you've never been on a bike in your life. Anyway, do you know how much a gym costs these days? You would be better trying to get more hours in the shop or find a job that pays real money.' He said the words with a smile on his face as though he was allowed to say anything so long as it was disguised as humour.

'Your golf club costs money and going out with the lads every weekend for a drink does too. You don't hear me complaining about it.' Her reply was said under her breath as though she knew the discussion might end in a row.

'Well when you bring in the same amount of money as I do then you too can take up golf, or bloody running, or whatever it is. Anyway, you know damn well this is all talk. Don't make me laugh, you always say these things and never do anything about it.' Lorna sighed; she had become used to her husband's cruel comments. She turned from the sink and looked at him as he wiped his mouth having finished his dinner.

'That's because every time I try to do something you either put me down or say it's too expensive or a waste of time.' Chick stood up and carried his empty plate over to the sink.

'Lori, I know I'm no David Beckham, but you are no supermodel either. Why can't you just be happy with what you have and stop always wanting to look for something else? For heaven's sake woman, admit you're old and accept it.' Charlie was indeed no David Beckham. Although he was still slim, he had a bulging pot belly that was more noticeable because of his lack of stature.

The conversation ended as it always did, in strained silence. Charlie would gradually feel guilty and eventually, he would try to placate his wife.

'Look, Lori, if you are really serious about taking up something to occupy your time then find out how much it will cost, and we can see if it's affordable.' That was always the way with him. They had enough money for both to have hobbies, but he liked to keep control of everything. The way she dressed, the money she spent, and even the few friends she still kept. Maybe an observer watching from the outside might have concluded that it was Charlie who was insecure. On the few occasions they went out on a weekend together or on holiday it would be Lorna who would attract the looks of both men and women. He was aware of his diminutive height and would always insist that she wore flat shoes. It wasn't that he stopped her from getting dressed up and looking good, he was proud of his wife. Nevertheless, now the boys had left home Charlie could not help but focus his attention on keeping Lorna exactly where he wanted her to be. Looking after him and keeping in the background.

'Forget it Chick. You're probably right. What would I do at a gym anyway?' It would probably be full of youngsters jumping around to that awful techno music. Maybe I'll try and see if the shop can give me more hours. Do you want another cup of tea?' She spoke the words while being on autopilot, they meant nothing to her. Lorna was already counting down the hours until Chick either went to bed or left for work in the morning. Only then would she be able to get back to the man who meant everything to her.

Charlie looked up and watched his wife as she worked away at the sink with her back to him. He studied her for a few minutes without speaking, almost as if he was seeing a woman for the first time in years. The way he once looked at her before the boys came along. Something felt different, she was different. It had only been a few months since Charlie Junior had been the last to leave. He couldn't quite put his finger on it. She was acting indifferent towards him, as though she was no longer subservient and in his shadow. But rather than feeling as though she no longer cared, Charlie felt threatened. It was as though the indifference was a challenge to his authority, almost as though she was breaking free.

'Is everything ok Lori?' She turned around and smiled but her eyes showed no emotion.'

'Of course, dear, I'm fine. I just need to learn to keep adjusting to the fact that it's just the two of us. I miss the boys, the noise, the way they always kept me busy.' Charlie nodded in agreement.

'You do know that I still love you don't you Lori?' Her dead eyes squinted slightly.

'Of course, you do Charlie., of course, you do. Now do you want that cup of tea or not?'

Computer Sex

It was after eleven that evening before she finally got back on to her computer. It had been a few frustrating hours before Charlie finally went off to bed. Lorna made the usual excuse that she would not be able to sleep so would stay up and watch television for a bit. She knew that her husband usually read before putting the light out. At last, after checking for the umpteenth time she could finally no longer see the glow emanating from underneath the bedroom door. Her fingers excitedly opened the tablet and within seconds she was online. Once again, she could become Georgie, the woman she longed to be. Exciting, desired, independent, confident, everything that Lorna wasn't.

Georgie Girl- Sorry, he took ages to go to bed my darling. Please tell me you are still up.

Rory- Still here my gorgeous. I missed you. I hate this having to wait around all day until you can get free of him.

Georgie Girl- I know my love. We will meet soon; I just know we will.

Rory- We will Georgie, we will. I have something I need to ask you.

Georgie Girl- Yes darling, anything. What is it?

Rory- I hate to bring the subject up again but you know my situation. Have you got any further with sending the cheque?

Georgie Girl- I'm almost there darling. He controls all our money and I've not used my personal account for years. It took a while to sort out getting it re-activated. I'm still waiting for some of the money to come in from the stuff I sold on eBay. Give me a few more days and it will be on its way.

Rory- I love you, Georgie. I'm so sorry to have to ask you to send me money but this £500 will keep the wolves from the door until that bitch pays me what I'm due. One day when we finally get together then Dyleekin Lodge will be all yours as well. We can make love every day you gorgeous creature.

Georgie Girl- I know my darling. I should be able to transfer the money in a few days. Did I tell you that I'm naked at the moment?

I will leave the rest of the texting conversation to your imagination as once again things became rather steamy between lonely Georgie and her digital lover Rory. Their passionate love affair had escalated very quickly to constant texts as well as some live video calls when the circumstances allowed it. The couple had exchanged plenty of photographs, many of rather a vivid nature. Georgie was smitten by the rugged Scotsman in his kilt and sometimes a lot less. How could she not fall for the handsome six feet muscle man who was everything Charlie was not? He was even a few years younger than her at 47 and could be considered as her toy boy. What was £500 when it came to being in love?

One Big Payday

'It's just a feeling I get, she's acting differently but I can't say how exactly.' Tina sat up in the bed and pulled a cigarette out from the packet sitting on the cabinet beside her. She chuckled self-consciously.

'Maybe she has always been like that, but you're just noticing her for once.' Charlie sensed the sarcasm in her voice and didn't like it. It was bad enough his wife acting strangely but his mistress being smart was too much for him.

'What the hell do you mean by that?' Tina knew she had gone too far. She sidled up to him playfully as he sat on the edge of the bed buttoning his shirt up. The young woman was naked, her face still flushed red from the exertion.

'Jesus Chick, I'm just teasing you. What's eating you up Mister Grumpy?' He smiled and then laughed before kissing her affectionately on the cheek.

'You ok for money; I mean do you need help with anything? Did his maintenance money come through again this month?' Tina nodded and gave him a rueful smile.

'Yeh, it did. Not that I'm going to be living it up with what that useless bastard pays me. Jack will need a whole outfit for starting school soon, those bloody things cost a fortune.' Charlie knew the game. He always felt obliged to give her money, even more so when they had just had sex. Their affair had been a sporadic thing. He would see her every few weeks and knew that she was seeing other men. He had a genuine affection for her though and he was sure that she felt the same.

'I'll transfer over a few hundred to your account when I get home later, love.' Tina smiled and playfully pulled him close before kissing him on the lips.

'You're too good to me Charlie boy. I don't deserve you, I really don't.'

That was the thing about Tina, she probably didn't deserve Charlie, but he deserved her, very much so. That evening she sat with her supposedly estranged partner Big Leckie checking payments coming into their bank account.

'Who was it today? Was it Charlie McGarvey? He just paid in £300.' Tina nodded as though she was bored.

'Yes, it was him today. Bobby Hamilton tomorrow and then the next one is Ike Hasslet next Wednesday.' Big Leckie turned and looked at her, a frown forming on his face.

'Next fucking Wednesday! You're slowing up girl, we need to get more customers. I thought we agreed on one a day.'

'I'm doing my fucking best Leck, I'm supposed to be in love with these losers, I can't just tell them when they can come here, they're all married. One of these days we will push it too far and half a dozen of them will all turn up at once.' She said the words softly, making sure not to anger her boyfriend. Big Leckie was not a man to be messed with. He treated her well and usually kept his temper, but it did not take much to turn him into a snarling raging bull. 'It's hard to keep track of them all when they text. I mean yesterday I called Bobby Ike or was it the other way around.'

'You're doing fine doll. Just keep the money coming in and we'll get by. Maybe we'll get a wee holiday in Majorca this year. Take Jack before he starts school.' Tina had heard this speech countless times. Maybe Big Leckie meant it when he said the words, but they each knew that their habit was what the money was for. Both of them were drug addicts but so far Tina had held back from following him and using needles.

Big Leckie switched the computer off and walked towards the kitchen before stopping and turning back around to face her. 'Do you think any of these guys are in love with you? I mean really going for it.' She shrugged her shoulders before replying.

'Maybe the guy today, Charlie. I've been screwing him the longest.'

'How about you do him over big time? Try to get him to pay big money, a one-off. Then we tell him to fuck off. What's he going to do? He can hardly go to the cops and spill the beans as his missus will find out. What do you think, Tina?

'I could try, I suppose.' She pulled a cigarette out of the packet on the table and lit it up before continuing. 'Are you going to skin up, I need a fix bad?' Big Leckie resumed his walk into the kitchen to get his stash. He sat down at the table and started to roll a cannabis joint that he would lace with heroin for Tina.

'Do you like him, this Charlie guy? I mean we could start with him and see if it comes off. If it does then maybe, we could try working on all of them for a big payoff. Instead of this few hundred pounds every few weeks from the losers, we go for the jackpot.' Tina had only caught the start of Big Leckie's speech, the bit about liking Charlie.

'Are you fucking kidding? Guys a baldy wee midget who stinks of BO. Always good at paying up though.'

The New Woman (Three months later)

Things had intensified over the last few months for Lorna or Georgie as she was known to her digital lover. During the day when Chick was at work, they would have live video calls, but the late evening ones would still have to be by text.

Georgie sat in the living room in her dressing gown with her hair tied up in a bun. The video calls meant she had to put her make-up on and look good for Rory, but it had started to cause friction between her and Chick. A few times he had come home early and wondered why she was making such an effort to look good. She had brushed it off by saying it was for him as she hoped to rekindle their spark, but her husband seemed neither flattered nor convinced. On the few occasions he approached her for sex she would make an excuse about feeling unwell or tired. She found it odd that he had been ignoring her for the last few years but was suddenly taking an interest again.

Rory- Oh God, I love you so much. I can't believe you would do this for me. You really are my dream woman.

Georgie Girl- It's alright my darling, I love you and I'll do anything for you.

Rory- Did they say exactly when the money would be in your account and available for transfer? I hate to pressure you, but this is a matter of life or death. As soon as the lawyers agree on what she owes me I will pay you the whole 10k back and more.

Georgie Girl- I don't care about the money. Just promise me that we can stick to the agreed date and I can leave him in two weeks for good.

Rory- Of course, of course, my Georgie. Once I have the money then Dyleekin Lodge is safe until she pays up. Our house, our home, together forever.

While the two internet lovers were getting it on, upstairs Charlie was in bed but unable to sleep. He had an important work meeting with his boss in the morning and he knew it was going to be a difficult conversation. For years he had made his targets and been well rewarded by the company. The last few months though had been a disaster. He had sold nothing and knew he had to turn things around quickly. The problem was he could not concentrate on his work because of the two women in his life. Suddenly from being in control he was now the one who felt insecure in both relationships. Tina had not been replying to his texts for weeks since he had given her the 10k loan. The agreement had been that she would repay him £50 a week but so far nothing. It was not as though he expected her to pay all the money back but to ignore his texts!! Something was wrong and now he had received a one-line message from her saying, *come to mine at 2 p.m. tomorrow.* Who the hell did she think she was?

And yet it was not Tina who was unsettling him, it was her, Lorna. Since Charlie Junior had left, she had become a different person. Before she had always been subservient and respectful. It wasn't as though she was rude or mean towards him, it was her aloofness, almost as though he no longer meant anything to her. Charlie had even tried fussing over Lorna, he brought flowers home one evening, but she simply smiled before quickly placing them in a vase in the kitchen. It was as though both he and the flowers were invisible. He knew something was going on. She now slept either on the sofa or in one of the spare bedrooms and had also taken to making herself look good. When he had jokingly asked who she was dressing up for she had replied, *for you Chick, who else would it be for?* Despite this, she was deliberately keeping him at arms-length. That was the thing, he was starting to realise just how attractive his wife still was.

Charlie wondered if she was talking to someone as she would disappear with her phone. He managed to get a hold of it a few times, but she had locked the screen. When he had asked her if something was going on and did, she still love him the answer had always been the same. *Of course, I do, what a ridiculous thing to ask.* The tone of the reply was dead and flat as though the question meant nothing to her. *What the hell was happening to him?*

Meet in the Middle

The black BMW was speeding through the tight streets of Dumfries as it headed towards one of the less affluent housing estates on the edge of the town. At the wheel was an angry little man. The meeting with his boss had not gone well for Charlie. He had managed to keep his temper and said very little but the implication that he was not concentrating on his work had stung. *All these years of giving everything I could and that is the thanks I get.* The reality was that Charlie had hardly been listening. He knew that the only way to be able to put the focus back on his work was to get these two stroppy bitches back in their cages. *How dare they treat him like this? He was the guy with the good job, the man with the money.* He was about to tell them both some home truths whether they liked it or not.

Normally when visiting Drumcree Crescent he would be more discreet and park his car a few streets away. Not this time. With a screech of brakes, he drove straight onto Tina's driveway and jumped out. Within seconds he was banging aggressively on the front door of the scruffy little terraced house. She took a few minutes to answer before opening it just enough to peer out at him. The young woman was still in her dressing gown and looked as though she had just crawled out of her bed. His anger was increasing by the second and so was his blood pressure.

'Tina, what the fuck do you mean by ignoring my texts? I want my bloody money back and I want it now. What the hell is wrong with you?' He suddenly realised that this might not be the best way to win her round and took a step back before continuing. 'Look Tina, love. What's going on, are you ok?' It was at that point that a new face replaced that of the young woman. Big Leckie was standing at the now wide-open door. He had his massive tattooed arms folded in front of him and towered over the diminutive Charlie. 'Who the fuck are you and what are you doing at Tina's house?' These words were enough to make Big Leckie slowly step outside and close the door behind him.

'Who the fuck are you shouting at wee man. Calm

down and let me explain a few things to you.' Charlie was confused and angry.

'I, I'm a friend of Tina's, and what's it got to do with you anyway. Who the hell are you?'

The smaller man knew he had said too much as Big Leckie's face turned an angry shade of purple as he lunged forward. He grabbed Charlie by the lapels of his suit jacket and lifted the little man off his feet bringing their two faces within inches of each other. The mismatch was there for all to see but for the still confused Charlie, the reality of the situation had yet to sink in.

'I'm only going to tell you this once, and once only you baldy little prick. Tina wants nothing to do with you anymore, so sling your hook and don't come back. Do you fucking hear what I'm saying, wee man?' As Big Leckie spoke the words he sprayed Charlie's face with little drops of spit.

'But, who, who are you?' Charlie spluttered the words out in shock.

'I'm Tina's husband, have been for fucking years.' Finally, the penny sank in with Charlie. The realisation that he had been conned was finally dawning on him. Unfortunately, it did not help him to say the right thing at the right time.

'Well, you tell Tina, I want my money back now, all of it. She, she can forget any payment plan we agreed on. I want the whole lot of it repaid and right now.' Big Leckie lifted Charlie up a few inches more and then with a frightening savage intensity he smashed his forehead into the smaller man's face before dropping him to the ground. Charlie rolled about on the grass in stunned agony as blood poured from his nose. He looked up at the towering Leckie just as the big man sent a boot straight into his victim's groin.

'We have no fucking idea what money you are on about, now get the fuck off my property before I do you some real damage.' With that, the big man nonchalantly turned around and walked back into the house. A stunned Charlie sat on the patchy grass and weeds trying to compose himself. He was sure that his nose was broken, and blood was dripping from his mouth. It was his pride though that hurt the most. He had been taken for an utter fool and he knew there was no way back on this one.

Charlie staggered back into his car and tried to wipe away the blood from his face. He suddenly became aware that his phone was ringing and without thinking he pressed receive. 'Charlie, where the hell are you? I've been trying to get a hold of you for ages. Your clients have all been calling saying you've missed their meetings. Charlie, you can't do this, you are going to lose the company big money. I thought we had agreed at our discussion that you would…' He switched the phone off and reversed the car quickly out of Tina's drive. There was only one thing on his mind now. The only way to stop everything from falling apart was to get back home to Lorna. Tell her he loved her and rebuild his life from the mess he was in.

Charlie was surprised to find the house empty on his return. He knew that this was her day off from the shop, but she had told him that she would just stay in and do housework. He stared at the small pile of letters on the floor and bent down to pick up one addressed to Mrs. Lorna McGarvey. Without any hesitation, he ripped open the envelope and read the words. At first, he was confused when he saw that it was a bank statement. *I thought she had cancelled this account years ago when I told her to.* But his confusion soon turned to shock when he studied the figures and found that she had taken out a £10,000 loan. But that was not the worst of it. He stared in disbelief when he read that the account was now empty, and the money had been transferred out.

Charlie was suddenly aware of the sound of a car pulling up outside the house. He dropped the letter and turned around in a daze to look out of the still-open front door. Lorna stepped from the driver's seat of the blue Ford Focus and nonchalantly walked up the garden path. She had an air of confidence in the way she carried herself. The make-up and tight jeans with a fitted white top made it obvious that she was dressed up to meet someone.

'Oh my God, what on earth happened to you?' She said the words, but her face seemed unconcerned, as though he was not there.

'Never fucking mind what happened to me, where the hell did you get that car and what the fuck are you doing taking out £10,000 bank loans? Have you lost your mind woman?' She simply brushed passed him and walked into the house. He followed her into the kitchen like a scalded puppy, confusion and disbelief overwhelming him. 'Lorna, will you please tell me what is going on?' She ignored him and bent down to pick up the handle of the large travel bag that sat on the kitchen floor.

'I'm leaving you Chick; I'll contact a lawyer at some point, and we can work out what you owe me.' She started to head back out the door, but Charlie managed to pull himself together and stood in her way.

'Are you going fucking crazy? Where the hell can you possibly go? You're not getting a penny off me you stupid bitch, you had better reconsider what the hell you're doing.'

'I'm going to stay with Rory, my lover. He has a Lodge in the Highlands; now could you please get out of my way.' Charlie was losing his temper and went to raise his hand to strike his estranged wife. She took a few steps back and suddenly her demeanour was no longer calm as her voice cracked with anger.

'Don't you dare, Chick, don't you dare. Now get out of my way, there is nothing you can do anymore. I don't hate you; I just don't care about you any longer. It's over, you need to accept that. Surely this can't come as a surprise to you

Chick, for God's sake. We have hardly spoken in years.'

Chick was no longer an angry little man. His whole world was crashing down around him. Tina, his job, the head-butt from Big Leckie, and now Lorna. He fell to his knees and started crying before looking up imploringly at his wife.

'Lori darling, please don't leave me. You're all I have, I'm sorry I've not been close to you over the last few years. It was just that the job took up so much time. Have I not always worked hard for you and the boys? Given you all you needed, a house, security, please Lori, you're being unfair.' She looked at him and shook her head.

'Why don't you go and move in with that young floozy you've been screwing for years, Chick? I'm sure she'll welcome you with open arms. Did you think I was so stupid that I didn't know what was going on? Do you seriously think I haven't noticed the amount of money you constantly post to her account? You may think I'm dumb Chick but it's only now that the boys are away that I'm confident enough to tell you to go to hell.' For once Charlie was lost for words and kept quiet while she spoke. 'Now, I need to get on the road. I would get that face of yours checked out; your nose might be broken.' She refrained from asking him what had happened but somehow, she sensed it was something to do with his mistress. Lorna brushed passed the broken man and walked out to the hire car while Charlie stayed kneeling in the doorway. He then wept uncontrollably to the sound of the blue Ford Focus disappearing into the distance.

The Chase

Lorna had now become Georgie full-time. She felt like a completely different woman as she stood in the lay-by smoking a cigarette while leaning on the bonnet of the hire car. In the distance, she could hear the roar of traffic passing by on the motorway. She was in no hurry to get to her lover at Dyleekin Lodge and had taken the old A74 road North rather than the quicker road that ran parallel. She pondered her future and smiled contentedly as a train sped passed on the adjacent railway line making its way North to Glasgow. All around her the green hills and trees stood tall and proud. Monuments to a future of independence and freedom.

Finally, she pressed her phone and watched as the screen jumped into life. The man of her dreams was staring back within seconds, his face smiling with happiness.

'Hello lovely. I wasn't expecting you to call until later. How are you, my gorgeous girl?'

'Hi Rory, I just had to call you as I miss you so much. Plus, I have something important to tell you.'

'Ooh that sounds exciting, what is it? Oh, the bank transfer came through. Well done and thank you so much. Give me a few weeks and we will be together at long last. I just need to sort out her and that bloody money-grabbing lawyer she has.'

'That's what I wanted to tell you. We don't need to wait for another two weeks. I have to see you now; I hired a car this morning and I'm coming up. I've finally done it; I've left Chick for good.' Suddenly Rory's expression changed to one of shock and maybe even horror.

'No, no Georgie, it's too soon my love. The place is a mess and she is popping in and out getting her stuff moved from the lodge. Let's wait another few weeks, honestly, it's for the best.' Georgie laughed and brushed the hair away from her eyes.

'Rory, I'm already on my way. I left him; this is it. Even if I have to stay in a hotel, I don't care. Why wait any longer, you have the money now, that's everything sorted out. To hell with her, she has no right to demand anything from you anymore.'

'It's, it's not that. I just wanted to get everything looking good for you. Could you not just wait a few weeks my love? Honestly, just a couple of weeks more.'

The conversation ended ten minutes later with a concerned-looking Rory finally accepting that Georgie would be at Dyleekin Lodge that very evening. No matter how hard he tried to convince his internet lover to wait for a few more weeks, she would not change her mind. She could see the reluctance written all over his face despite attempts to disguise it. The old Lorna would have listened to him and turned around, but not Georgie. The new woman was making her own future and there could be no going back.

'Ok, ok Georgie. If you insist then we just need to go for it. Call me when you get to the village at Achnaculloch and I'll guide you to the Lodge. I, I love you. Drive carefully and see you soon.'

The blue Ford Focus indicated to pull out of the lay-by even though the road both ahead and behind was empty. The sun shone down from a clear blue sky as the freedom wagon restarted its journey to the Highlands. Each mile would take Georgie girl further away from her grim past to a bright new future, or that's what she hoped.

Charlie had finally managed to pull himself together. He showered and washed away the blood from his face before changing into casual joggers and a t-shirt. His lips were swollen from the punch and his nose was red but at least he could touch his face without wincing in pain. He hoped it might not be broken after all, but the reality was, he no longer cared. His phone continued to buzz as both his clients and boss tried desperately to contact him. Charlie looked at the screen and read the last of multiple messages that awaited his attention. *Charlie, you either get in contact NOW or you are going to be out of a job. Head office is going crazy and so are the clients.* He pressed block on his phone and placed it back into his pocket.

For the next few hours, Charlie turned the house upside down trying to find something to give him a clue about where his wife was heading too. She had taken the laptop with her but very little else. He emptied the drawer of paperwork on the floor and searched through each scrap but found little that would give him any idea as to what was going on. Finally, in a moment of despair, Charlie sat down on the sofa that his wife had slept on the previous evening. His hand rested beside him and touched something that made him turn and look. A tiny little notebook was jammed down the side of one of the cushions. He opened it with hope rather than expectation. Most of the writing seemed to be scribbles including shopping lists but some of the pages had love hearts drawn on them. Each one a different size, sometimes a few together and others with arrows through the centre. It was on the last page that he found what he was looking for. A big heart shape with a name written in the middle and further writing underneath. Rory, Dyleekin Lodge, Achnaculloch.

Barely three hours after his wife had left in the little blue Ford Focus the black BMW was also speeding North. Charlie was not letting Lorna go without a fight. His satnav told him it was 250 miles from Dumfries to Dingwall in the Highlands. He reckoned it would take her 6 or more hours to get there. He could do it in 4 if he kept his foot down. This was it; Charlie was going to get his life back on track or die in the attempt.

It was nearly seven in the evening when he pulled into the service area on the A9 just outside of Inverness. He had less than an hour to drive to the village of Achnaculloch and would have completed the journey nonstop if he had not been desperate to go to the toilet. As he stood relieving himself in the busy bathroom, it dawned on him how hungry and thirsty he was. Charlie had not eaten or drunk anything since leaving his house that morning.

A few minutes later he stood in the queue that snaked back to the edge of the restaurant. Just as he was on the verge of giving up Charlie spotted her, almost at the front of the queue. The shapely figure in the white top that he had ignored for so many years was now the object of his utmost attention. He immediately abandoned his place in the queue and pushed his way to the front. Almost everyone he brushed past made an angry comment, *oi, buddy, get to the back and wait your turn, hey, excuse me but there is a queue if you don't mind.* He ignored them all and grabbed Lorna's shoulder just as she handed over a pile of loose change for her coffee. She twirled around with the force of Charlie's hand sending the money and coffee crashing to the floor. Only it wasn't Lorna, it was someone else much younger. *How could he be so stupid? The woman looked nothing like his wife.* Unfortunately for Charlie two burly truck drivers were directly behind the woman he had accosted. They pinned him to the ground while the staff called the police. He tried desperately to explain that it was all a mistake, but the shocked crowd eyed him with both contempt and embarrassment. The final straw came when one of his captors shouted at him, 'Stay still you dirty wee sex pest creep. The police have been called and are on their way.'

It's maybe at this point that you might start to feel sorry for Charlie. I mean I know he is not the nicest bloke in the world but Jeez, give the man a break, did he really deserve all this? Yes, he probably did, and it took a good deal of explaining and apologising before he was allowed to go on his way. The police told him he might face charges, it depended on his victim. The poor woman was still in shock although she did accept that her assailant had mistaken her for someone else.

Charlie walked back to his car feeling like a beaten man, but he was still not going to give up. He felt calm now, surely things could not get any worse, this had to be rock bottom. He would plead, beg, and promise the world to Lorna if she would just take him back. Give him one last chance to prove he loved her and then they could rebuild their lives from all this mess. Somehow, he knew that his hope of achieving success was slim, just like his attempt to get a coffee had been.

The House in the Woods

Georgie edged the car slowly along the twisting little main street of Achnaculloch. She was surprised to see how small the settlement was. Ok, she had not been expecting to find a sprawling metropolis but somehow, she had conjured up visions of a large picturesque village nestled in between tall mountains and swaying fir trees. Dreams of her and Rory sipping drinks beside a roaring pub fire and taking morning coffee at one of the local cafés soon evaporated as she reached the last building within seconds. She parked the car beside a farm gate and walked back towards the houses. The place looked even uglier on foot. Just a single narrow street lined with low grey cottages and one small village store that doubled up as the Post Office being the sum total of the buildings. Even the surrounding land looked bland. Flat green fields and a few tired-looking trees. Achnaculloch was the sort of village you would drive through and forget within seconds.

Georgie pushed open the stiff door of the shop and walked inside. An old-fashioned bell tinkled in the background to warn the owner that a rare customer had arrived. Tins of beans, soup, toilet rolls, and toothbrushes lined the shelves. A middle-aged man with a beard and over large spectacles shuffled up behind the Perspex screen that covered half of the small counter. He had probably been a handsome man in his time but now he looked as though life had beaten him down. His untidy hair and baggy jumper gave the impression that he existed rather than lived. 'Post office business or shop?' He said the words in an abrupt but not unfriendly tone.

'Er, no neither if that's ok. I was just looking for some directions.' Georgie suddenly felt guilty asking for help without spending any money.

'Oh, actually, do you sell wine?' The man stepped away from the Perspex screen onto the other half of the counter that was open plan.

'Sorry madam, no license. No chance of the lonely wee shop owner getting a license. The big store in Dingwall can get one no problem, me, no chance. I'm trying to get a petition going, you know to get the locals and tourists to sign it. If I can get 1000 signatures, then they will have to reconsider my application. Maybe you would be interested in putting your name on it?'

'Oh, Ok, sorry to hear that. I'm in a bit of a hurry, maybe next time. I wonder if you could help me though. I was looking for a place called Dyleekin Lodge.' The man looked confused.

'Dyleekin what ?' Georgie suddenly felt embarrassed as she showed him a slip of paper that read, Rory Macintyre, Dyleekin Lodge Estate, Achnaculloch.' The shopkeeper lowered his spectacles to read the note and then looked up at Georgie with a smile on his face.

'Ahh, is that what he calls it now? It's always been known as Dulican farm around here, but he changes the name often. Well, that's assuming we are talking about the same Rory Macintyre. Be surprising if there were two of him.' The man looked Georgie up and down making it obvious that he liked what he saw. In the past, she might have felt embarrassed or even offended but the new Georgie was enjoying the attention.

'Oh, so you know Rory. That's good. Could you show me where he lives then?'

Despite seeming initially unfriendly the little shopkeeper insisted on taking her outside to give directions to her intended destination. 'You just need to go through that gate over there at the end of the village. Some idiot has blocked it with that blue car, but you can just walk up. Macintyre's place is about a quarter of a mile up the track. Take care and good luck.' He touched her arm as he said the words causing Georgie to turn around and look at him. His eyes smiled, she liked him, he seemed nice if rather odd.

'Thanks, thank you, and I hope you get a license to sell alcohol one day.' She went to move away but just as she did the shopkeeper had some final advice to give.

'Listen, be careful up there. I'm not a big fan of Mr. Macintyre, I don't think anyone in the village is. If you have any problems or need any help just call back into the shop.'

Georgie walked back towards the gate and her car. She took out the picture she held close to her heart of Rory looking tall and proud in his kilt. His greying beard and the waves of silvery hair made him look like the archetypical Highland Laird. Her fingers touched the phone she had in the pocket of her jeans, but she pulled back. Maybe it was intuition, could it be that she was unsure of what she might find? *No, come on Georgie girl, go up there and surprise him. Show him how clever I am finding my way to the Lodge without calling first.*

As she walked along the lightly worn track that edged beside a field a black BMW pulled up and parked behind the blue Ford Focus. Charlie stepped out of the car. He looked dishevelled and exhausted, the chase and the day's events had finally caught up with him. He looked around and then noticed the open gate. On one of the posts, he read the words Dulican farm. Somehow, he knew that this had to be the place. Charlie started to run up the track with the intent of reclaiming his wife. It was time for the showdown.

Georgie stood still and surveyed the scene before her. The path finally ended at a clump of overgrown shrubs and trees. What looked like it had once been a substantial house was now a crumbling ruin. Most of the structure stood only a few feet tall although the back wall remained almost at its full height. Part of the roof was still attached to it while the remainder lay in a pile of rubble at the side amongst the bushes and tall weeds. Some semblance of work seemed to have taken place at one time as half-built scaffolding balanced against the bigger wall. A rusting cement mixer and the rotting remains of a JCB digger and an old transit van completed the scene.

Georgie started to walk around towards the rear wall. It was at that point that she noticed the small dirty white caravan nestled at the back of the ruin. Someone was home as an old green Sierra was parked alongside. She edged gingerly through the weeds and junk and knocked on the door. A few seconds later it opened and in front of her stood a man who resembled Rory but did not really look like him. Maybe his face was the same, but he seemed much shorter than in his photographs. His hair was also whiter than she remembered. The handsome man in his kilt had been replaced by someone who looked very ordinary and unromantic. He was wearing a dirty yellow boiler suit and wellingtons. Rory looked shocked to see Georgie standing in front of him.

'I thought you agreed to call me. I would have got changed and put on some decent clothes to come down to the village and meet you.' He looked extremely uncomfortable, gone was the confident man she knew from the internet. 'Look, look, Georgie, I know this is not quite what you expected.' She stared at him and chuckled with embarrassment before replying.

'You can say that again, Rory. That's if you are Rory Macintyre as you don't look much like your photographs. What the hell is going on? Where is the lodge, we were going to live in? Please don't tell me this is it.' Georgie said the words almost mockingly, as though she was ready to burst into laughter. It was at this point that a red-faced Charlie arrived on the scene. Georgie spun round in surprise to see her errant husband standing behind her. He was gasping for breath with the exertion from running and had to bend down for a few seconds to collect himself. He finally looked up at the man opposite and then at his wife.

'So, this is what you left me for? A scruffy little nobody and a crumbling ruin?' Charlie was laughing now as he basked in his triumph. It was becoming clear to all that Lorna had been conned out of her money.

'What the hell are you doing here, Chick? This has nothing to do with you, please go.' At this point, Rory decided it was time to state his case.

'Yes, I want you both off my property. I told you not to come here Georgie, you wouldn't bloody listen. Just like her, you women are all the same. I was going to meet you in the village and tell you it was over between us.' Charlie looked at his wife with contempt and then walked over to within a few feet of Rory.

'Oh, she will be leaving all right and coming back home with me where she belongs. But first of all, you'll give me the money back that you stole from us. The stupid cow might be as gullible as they come but I'm not.' Georgie edged slowly away and watched the two little men square up to each other. She felt like laughing as she realised how alike they both were. Two small cheating little con men who thought they had won. Maybe she had known that her journey would end in disappointment from the moment she had told Rory that she was on her way. What did it matter? It had been a means to an end, a reason to leave her husband once and for all.

Rory was now red in the face as he stared back at Charlie.

'The money was gifted to me by your wife and it's now spent. It's got fuck all to do with you anyway as she was leaving you for me. Well, you can have her back for all I care, I got what I wanted.' Suddenly Charlie tried to throw a punch, but his wild swing only connected with fresh air. Within seconds the two men were rolling around in the grass trying to get hold of each other's throats.

Georgie was smiling as she walked back down the track towards her car. She had never felt happier or more free since she had been a child. For the first time in years, she belonged to no man. Not Chick, not Rory, now she was only answerable to herself. Yes, it was going to be hard explaining to the boys why their marriage was over. It might even mean moving back in with her ageing mother until she got a lawyer and sorted out the sale of the house and the money. She would get by; they would both get by. It was time to go home, go back to find the real Georgie.

She sat in her car and watched as Chick raced back down the track towards her. Georgie pressed the button to let the window down.

'Chick, don't you ever get the message. What the hell do you want now? Are you going to keep running after me for the rest of your life?' Charlie was covered in dirt, his lip was bleeding, and his nose was still swollen from the previous beating by Big Leckie.

'Lorna, you are coming home. Look please, I mean it, I forgive you all this, even the ten thousand pounds you have thrown away. You must come home now, for yourself and the boys.' She smiled back at him with a look of both compassion and sympathy.

'I already am home Chick. That saying, home is where the heart is. It's true because my heart left you a long time ago. My lawyer will be in touch. Be careful driving back to your house, you look a right state.'

She let the window close on her old life and turned the car around to head back south to her mother's place in Stranraer, a good 50 miles further than Dumfries. Charlie walked over to the BMW and sat in the driver's seat. His head slumped on the steering wheel. He took out his phone and stared at it for a few minutes before finally pressing his boss's number.

Georgie pulled the car to a stop outside the little store

in Achnaculloch. The shopkeeper peered over his glasses and smiled. He seemed pleased to see her back so soon. She picked up a few provisions for the long journey to the Borders and placed them on the counter in front of him. 'Can I have a bag as well please?'

'Have you travelled far?' She nodded her head at him.

'Oh, you have no idea how far I have come in the last few months.' He held out his hand to her.

'Dave, my name is Dave. I took over the shop some years back when I split from my wife. Seemed like a good idea at the time, you know living in a village, getting back to simplicity, all that stuff. I can't say it was my best move.' Georgie took his hand and shook it. 'I take it things did not go well with Rory Macintyre then?' She smiled at him before replying.

'Oh, things went fine with Mr. Macintyre. I just went to say goodbye, that's all. My name is 'Geor….no, I mean Lorna, my name is Lorna. I used to be Lorna McGarvey but I'm back to my maiden name, Lorna Ellis. Now, did you mention you wanted me to sign a petition for you?'

Woman

I see the sparkle in your eyes like those distant suns that refuse to die
The glimmer of life while hope shimmers through the blackened sky
I see the despairing victim of man's arrogance stand bruised but proud
The light in your eyes defiant as only woman can
I see the day that comes when your chains fall free
And you will walk tall again while your jailers cower lonely in corners to understand fear themselves.

The Watcher

Who in God's name am I? I know I have a body even though I cannot see or feel. I sense I have arms, legs, a head, and a face but I have no feeling, no reality. There is no sound and yet I stand on a hillside. Why is there no wind, no rain, why, why, why? The questions come while I stare out at the countryside below, I can't move, I can't touch, and yet I still have thoughts. A voice in my head pleading for an explanation. All around me the land seems to shimmer in some strange half-life. My peripheral vision is just fleeting shadows, a bleak rainbow of dirty colours merging and mixing before separating only to merge again.

And yet all this means nothing because I have one thing to cling to, even though it fills me with even more dread. I am almost blind until I find the one, I must watch. Then and only then does my vision become perfect. Every other sense is dead and bleak, but I can see with absolute clarity the person that I seek. How long have I been doing this? One hour, one day, one year? It doesn't matter, I am doomed to stare out into the distance at that single individual. I have no clue who it is and why I must see their every move so clearly. There are so many questions but no one to answer even one of them.

Maybe I am dead but what would be the point of this torture making me watch a stranger go about their normal life? I cannot hear but a soft voice is floating in my brain quietly repeating the same words over and over again. It tells me who I am, what I am. Even if I have to answer my own questions, I will whisper to myself until I finally understand. And slowly, ever so slowly it starts to make sense and my despair is complete. I am not dead but how I wish I was. This is a fate far worse than death for now at last I know my name. They call me The Watcher, the one who brings death.

* * *

John Graham pulled the peaked cap further over his forehead as he looked towards the low hills. They seemed to swallow the lines of shiny steel as they reflected the late afternoon sun back towards the blue sky. He had been through this ritual a thousand times and just accepted it as something he would always do until his working days ended. Now each time he saw the wisp of white smoke float out from one of the distant hills it was as if a clock had ticked off another step towards midnight.

The railway had always been a part of the Graham family for as long as he could remember. His grandfather had held the high position of station master at the large nearby country town of Dumfries. John's father Robert had followed in his footsteps to take over the lonely outpost of Blackcraig station, a position he held for more than thirty years. It had been a proud day when his son had been promoted through the ranks to run the same station. John often thought back to that day in 1952 when the staff had stood on the platform to applaud Robert as he handed over the keys to his boy. And yet the little ceremony had been tinged with a more melancholic air than it would usually have been. They all knew that change was coming. Pat the signalman, wee Arthur the junior porter, and old Hugh the assistant station master, each one wondering if this would be the last new boss they would welcome.

The days of the country railway were coming to an end, even more so in the lightly populated Galloway hills of South West Scotland. So far a few of the branch lines to the more remote villages had succumbed but the Port line still clung on. And now ten years later it still threaded its way through the trees and valleys taking the once-a-day express boat train from London onto the ferry port of Stranraer. The rest of the traffic was made up of a few local trains and the occasional goods train. As the mid-1960s approached only John and the new signalman Davy Sedgwick were still employed at this remote outpost. But for how much longer would that last?

The hissing black steam engine clanked to a stop at the

platform, the wheels of its three maroon-coloured carriages squealing as they rattled to a stop. John walked over towards the cab for a quick chat with Josh McPake the train driver who smiled out from the engine, his arms folded over the edge of the side window. 'How goes it Josh, that wife of yours still giving you grief then?' The good-natured tone of the potentially rude question made it obvious that the two men shared in the joke.

'Aye, still moaning that I don't look like Cary Grant.' They laughed at the ridiculous comparison. Old Josh was bald and rotund but was a well-known character on the railway. He was a man who was respected and liked by all. 'How's the youngster, any better?' At first, John was confused but then he remembered his last conversation with Josh regarding the new signalman, Davy Sedgwick.

'Oh aye, young Davy. No, still the same. Wet behind the ears and can't think for himself. Och, but he's harmless enough, just a gormless young man.' Josh nodded his head as he listened. He had heard the same words spoken by most of the older employees on the line during the last few years. As each of the old school retired, they would either be replaced by inexperienced youngsters or in some cases not at all. This was the very reason why John now ran Blackcraig without an assistant or a porter.

'You still not going to take a day off and make it to the Blackcraig Gala next week?' Josh asked the question knowing only too well that John would never take a Saturday holiday. Like his father and his father's father before him, John was proud that he had never lost a day while working on the railway. He would take his two weeks of annual leave each year and his free day on a Sunday and that would be it.

'No, I'll come along after I finish work although no doubt by that time the drinkers and the louts will have taken over for sure.' Josh nodded his head and started to turn back towards the levers and dials inside the cab of the engine.

'It's a shame as I'm sure that lovely wife of yours Jean and wee Donnie would love to see you at the afternoon procession.'

There was no time for further conversation as the train was required to run to a strict timetable. John blew the whistle that hung around the starched white collar of his uniform as Josh busied himself inside the cab and the train slowly hissed away from the platform. The very reason why all their jobs were being threatened was there for all to see. Not a single person had got on or off the train. Maybe a few would at some of the bigger towns and villages along the way but not at Blackcraig. Like the other smaller stations, it suffered from the increase in private car ownership that had occurred since the end of the war. It also had the added disadvantage of being four miles from the actual village it was supposed to serve. The few potential customers that remained had mostly deserted to the more convenient buses that went through the centre of the towns.

John walked down the platform towards the small neat buildings that housed the ticket office and the waiting room of the isolated country station. An ornate lattice footbridge crossed the two main railway tracks over to the second platform that was used for trains coming back from Stranraer towards Dumfries. The signal box was situated on that side of the station and he could see young Davy leaning out of the window with a mug of tea in his hand. Both men would have little to do for the next two hours until another train rattled through their lonely outpost and broke the silence. It irked John that he would spend the intervening hours tending the plant pots and sweeping the platforms of the compact country station, while the youngster would do little to help. The old staff had respected the station master and needed no encouragement to busy themselves during the quiet periods between trains. Maybe it was the comment from Josh that had gotten to him, but John decided to have another attempt to bring the youngster into line. Rather than head back into the station building he instead walked over the footbridge towards the signal box.

'Alright Mr. Graham, how goes it?' The words were said in a disinterested rather than disrespectful tone.

'Davy, I thought maybe you could give me a hand if you want. The flower baskets need to be watered and I still have to brush this platform as well.'

'Sorry boss, I'm not allowed to leave the box in case another train gets put through.' John felt a slight flush of anger at these words. He was normally a calm individual who rarely lost his cool, but he knew that the young signaller was deliberately goading him. The fact that a relative newcomer to the railway was trying to tell the station master how to run his station was a step too far.

'Don't talk daft Davy, the next train is not due for a few hours yet, you know that.'

'Yes, but they might send a goods through and I would maybe even have to shunt it into the sidings. Anyway boss, you know it's against the rules for me to leave my post.' John involuntarily looked over to the goods sidings at the back of the station. They rarely saw any traffic and the tracks stood empty and overgrown with long grass. The comment from the youngster was deliberately mischievous and suddenly he became aware that he had maybe pushed the easy-going station master too far. Before John could respond the young man quickly fired off a question in the hope of deflecting any potential confrontation.

'First passenger we've had from the mid-afternoon train this week boss, although I never saw him get out of the carriage.' John had just been about to have a go at Davy, but the comment took him off his guard.

'What are you talking about? No one got on or off. I was standing talking to Josh, there was not a soul got off that bloody train. Are you trying to be smart with me, Davy?' The thought that he had missed a passenger leaving the train was a slight against his pride. John was proud of his role as station master and would have been mortified to not have noticed if someone had left one of the carriages and he had not asked for their ticket.

'Yes, boss. I never saw him get off but when the train pulled out, he was standing at the end of the platform, just over there.' He pointed to the spot he was talking about and John's eyes followed the direction of his finger.

'Are you sure, are you just kidding me, Davy? Don't mess me around boy, I can take a joke but don't push it.' He said the words sharply and the youngster's face went red with embarrassment as he realised, he had now annoyed the usually placid and calm John.

'I swear to God Mr. Graham, tall guy, he was wearing a long black coat and a fedora hat pulled down over his face. I thought that was who you were walking towards as the train pulled out. That's why I was surprised that you came over the footbridge instead.'

∗ ∗ ∗

John finished writing the day's business into the station ledger as the clock ticked towards six-thirty in the evening. The takings for the day had been pitiful once again.

Three parcels delivered, two dispatched, one wagon of coal dropped off from the mid-day local goods train, and three passenger tickets sold for the morning train to Dumfries. He knew he should have been thinking about the future and how he would find work if and when they finally decided it was no longer worth running the station at Blackcraig. But it was his pride that was hurting. *What if young Davy had been telling the truth and he had let a passenger through his station without collecting his ticket?* It was almost as if he could feel the eyes of both his father and his grandfather looking down at him and shaking their heads with disapproval. Both men were long dead, but he knew they would never have let a customer leave a train without them knowing about it. It was the golden rule of everything the role of station master stood for.

John closed the book and smiled. *Och, for God's sake man get a grip. That young eejit is just winding you up. Don't be so daft. How the hell would I not have seen a supposedly tall man leave an empty train? Anyway, surely Josh would have mentioned it. Yes, that's it, I can ask Josh tomorrow when he comes through again, that'll shut the youngster up once and for all.*

'Goodnight Boss, catch you tomorrow.' John watched as Davy grabbed his coat from the hook on the ticket office door and hurried out to the waiting car. He lived a few miles away at Rowantree farm with his parents and would finish at the same time as the station master. The signal box would be switched out and the station closed even though at least one evening train would pass through non-stop. The railway was being run down as an economic measure, another sure sign that the end might be coming.

John locked the door and walked over to the motorbike that lay propped up against the open gate into the small station car park. It would only take him ten minutes to ride down the winding little road back to the village of Blackcraig. By seven o'clock he would be home and back with the two most important people in the world to him, Jean and wee Donnie his three-year-old bundle of pure joy.

John turned the ignition key and place his foot on the starter peddle of the 1958 Ariel Leader motorcycle. The engine kicked into life as he watched the car disappear further down the road with Davy and his father in it. It made him feel inadequate. Here was the station master, a once respectable job and all he could afford was a motorbike. John would have loved to own a car but the threat to the railway and his future made him insecure about spending a lot of money. He had his family to look after and nothing else mattered.

It was just as he was about to turn the throttle of the machine and head out of the entrance that something made him swing around and look back at the building. The top of the footbridge could just be made out as it climbed above the roof of the station. Someone was standing on the stairs looking back at him. He knew instantly who it was as he recollected the description young Davy had given him of the passenger who had left the mid-afternoon train. John refused to lose his cool, he was the station master, always in control, ready to uphold the tradition of the Graham family no matter the situation. He turned the engine of the motorbike off and propped it back against the wall.

'Hey, excuse me, Sir. Can I help you?' He shouted the words as he tried to walk calmly back towards the building. Within seconds he was on the platform but to his surprise the footbridge was empty. John spent the next fifteen minutes searching every room in the station but there was no sign of the stranger. He finally gave up and headed back to his motorbike. And yet despite finding nothing he could still sense the presence of someone or something watching him.

It was a confused man who drove down the road back to Blackcraig that evening. For the first time in his life, he no longer felt in complete control. The trains might run to a strict timetable and life would meander on as normal in this little forgotten part of the country, but a change was coming. The truth was maybe it had already arrived.

* * *

John could tell that Jean was not her usual self. It

was hard to put his finger on exactly why, but he sensed a heavily disguised nervousness as she busied herself getting the evening meal ready. Little Donnie was climbing onto his father's knees and trying to pull the railway cap off his head. Few would have recognised the usually austere station master who patrolled the platform at Blackcraig as he relaxed with his child. John sat at the table with his shirt open, the jacket of his uniform hanging up in the hall. Each evening when he came home from work he would go through the same ritual with his boy. The youngster would try to remove his father's hat and John would tease him by pulling away just as the little one got close. The squeals and laughter of both young and old would keep Jean smiling as she prepared the food.

It wasn't until later that evening that John understood why his wife had been quieter than usual. Donnie had finally gone to sleep after his father read him the same story the child demanded each evening. Jean stood up from her seat beside the fire and walked over to the table in the hall. She lifted the phone book and brought the letter that had been concealed underneath it over to her husband. Neither said a word as he took the envelope in his hands without opening it and looked into her eyes. He could see the fear and sadness reflecting back at him. 'Railway business then?' It was a pointless question as he already knew that it would be.

'Yes, from head office in Glasgow. I had to sign for it.' John dropped the letter on the table and stood up before walking over to his wife. He took her in his arms and pulled her closer.

'Don't fret my love. If it's the closure notice for Blackcraig then they will just move me along to the next open station on the line. It might mean a longer journey on that old motorbike, but we can get through whatever life throws at us. I love you and wee Donnie too much to let something like this get in our way. Trust me, darling I'll always look after our family.' Jean held him tightly as though she was afraid to let him go.

'I know John, but for how long? The other stations are bound to follow and then it'll be the whole railway closing.' He let her go and walked back over to the table before lifting the letter with an air of resignation.

'We have at least another five years left. They can't close the whole line yet; it's still needed for the boat train from London. They won't want to upset the bigwigs down South. Even if the locals no longer use the line it's still needed. They would never divert the express through Kilmarnock, it's far too long that way.' He was just about to rip open the letter when the next words Jean spoke made him drop it to the floor in shock.

'There was a strange-looking man came to the door today, just before you got home. Weirdest thing ever.' John waited for her to continue with a growing sense of unease.

'Yes, just after Jack the postie came with the letter, the

doorbell went again, and I thought it was Jack coming back.'

'Go on, so who was it?'

'Well that's the thing, I don't know who it was, he never spoke.' John was standing stock still; he could feel every nerve in his body tense up.

'I opened the door and there was this really tall man standing at the top of the path. He was wearing a long coat and a hat pulled down over his face. He never said a word, he just turned and walked off into the village. He gave me the creeps if I'm being honest. I got the impression he was looking for someone.'

John had a worried frown on his face as he picked up the envelope and ripped it open without saying anything further. He read the words written in ink on the official 'British Railways' headed notepaper. Jean could feel her eyes well up with tears as she saw the look on his face change to one of shock.

* * *

It was a long wait the following day until the 4:22 local to Stranraer came through. John had to spend his time trying to placate young Davy Sedgwick, even his mother wanted a chat about what the future might hold. The handful of passengers who still used Blackcraig station had also heard the news and wanted to hear his opinion. Each train that stopped had seen an enquiring driver or guard desperate to talk about the bleak situation. And yet, all of it had meant little to John. He needed to speak to Josh to prove to himself that the tall man had not left the train yesterday. If he could sort that out, then hopefully it would allow him to focus on the dreadful news that the letter of the previous evening had brought.

At long last, he could see the wisp of steam rising above the cutting in the distance. The syncopated beat of the steam engine could be heard as it toiled its way up the gradient towards Blackcraig. Unlike the sun of yesterday, the gloom had descended, and low-lying clouds were sending damp relentless rain onto the platforms and buildings of the little station. Maybe even the weather had heard the bad news and had decided to join in the sad atmosphere that hovered over the setting.

The engine finally pulled up alongside the platform and clattered to a halt. John tried to keep calm, but he could feel the tightness in the pit of his stomach. Josh leaned out and spoke before the station master was even alongside. 'Bloody disgrace. How the hell can they make a decision like that, they don't care a jot about the lives it will impact.' John decided to go with the flow and let Josh have his rant before asking him the only question he cared about.

'I know, I know Josh. It's awful news, not what any of us were expecting at all.' Josh shook his head and then looked back along the platform to see if he was clear to go.

'I mean I expected them to close a few stations John, and sorry to say it Blackcraig would have been high on the list, but Jesus, the whole line to go next year. We are all fucked, no way can they find jobs for all of us. It might mean moving to Glasgow or worse, across the bloody border to England. Carlisle or maybe even Newcastle.' Josh was already turning to look forward, his hand on the lever to set the engine in motion. John quickly checked the empty platform and then edged back up to the cab for a last word with the driver. But he was too late as Josh had now moved over to the controls on the other side of the engine and the sound of hissing steam meant he could no longer be heard. In desperation, John shouted at old Blacky the fireman who was busy shovelling coal into the blazing fire of the mechanical monster.

'Blacky, Blacky, did you notice anyone get off the train yesterday? I mean get off here, at Blackcraig?' The question obviously confused the old man as he stood up and gave John a puzzled look.

'Whit, ye mean aff this train?' The engine was now moving forward, and John had to walk alongside to try and catch the words.

'Yes, this train, did anyone get off yesterday.' Blacky leant out of the cab window as the engine and carriages picked up speed.

'Aye, do you mean the same guy who just got aff the

noo. Him doon there, at the end of the platform. Must have got oan while the train waited at Dumfries. This is the only time I've seen him. Same as yesterday, he just appears when we get to Blackcraig.' Blacky shouted a final parting joke as the train chugged away. 'You losing your touch John, a rare customer at your station and ye missed him.'

The mixture of lingering engine smoke and damp rain made it difficult to see the end of the station clearly. John stared transfixed as he waited for it to clear. His worse fears were confirmed when he looked back at an empty platform. The man whoever he might be was no longer there. Somehow, he knew that a search would prove to be fruitless. He couldn't ask young Davy if he had seen the man again without making a fool of himself. For the first time in his life, the station master no longer felt in control. He was normally a calm God-fearing man who liked things to be organised and ordered. Just like the trains that ambled along the railway day in and day out and always worked to a strict timetable. Now everything was changing. The line was going to be axed and his young family would have to leave the village of Blackcraig if he was to find work. More than seventy years of service from his grandfather, father, and John himself was been tossed into the wind. And yet the only thing that the station master could think of was the tall man who had alighted at his station. The man who had visited his house and knocked on the door. *Who the hell was he and why was he playing these strange games with him?* John Graham was not someone to be messed with. He would get to the bottom of this no matter the cost.

※ ※ ※

It was the Friday evening before the Blackcraig Gala that John hatched his plan. A damp mist was shrouding the station, typical Scottish summer weather. The tall man had appeared twice more over the previous week, each time on different trains than the one that held Josh and his fireman Blacky. Of course, he would remain out of sight to the station master, it would be the young signalman Davy Sedgwick who would report seeing him. The conversation to convince Davy that he would have to leave his signal box to help out had been fraught. Even though the young man was in his early twenties he seemed immature for his age. 'But, Mr. Graham you know that is against the rules while a train is in the station.' The confused and now slightly scared youngster tried to reason with the normally placid station master. 'Look, John, I mean, Mr. Graham, I promise I, I'll help sweep up and look after the plants. I can do that when a train is out of my section. I just can't leave the box when a train is in, you know that.' John had lifted the boy off his feet and pulled him close to his now red and angry face.

'You're not listening to me, Davy. I'm in charge here at

Blackcraig. If I bloody well tell you to leave your post, then you bloody well leave your post. Do I make myself clear?' For a minute it looked as though the signalman was about to burst into tears.

'Ok, Ok, Mr. Graham. I'll do as you ask, it's just that they told me during my training never to leave the box if a train was in my section, that's all. I'm just following what they told me, Mr. Graham, sir. What they told me.' John had felt a tinge of guilt at that point and let go of the now snivelling young man.

'Look, Davy. I need you to do this for me. We can't have someone making a fool out of us and not handing their ticket over. I mean the guy might not even be paying for his ticket and that's defrauding the railway. Anyway, surely you do realise, we are all going to lose our jobs next year. Every last one of us will either be on the dole or have to move to find work. Do you really think everyone else on the Port line will be sticking to the rules? The place is finished, can't you understand that?'

It was raining once more as the train pulled up alongside the platform. John could sense the feeling of sadness that permeated the surroundings. Within twelve months the station would lay empty. The tracks would be torn up and after more than one hundred years the hills would fall silent. No longer would the sheep run to the opposite sides of the fields as the 2:45 to Stranraer trundled by. No more would the farmer hear the whistle of the local goods train as it clanked its way around the overgrown station sidings picking up its meagre fare.

John watched intently as the engine steamed away. He could see Davy standing at the other end of the platform with his arms outstretched and his head shaking. It was just as the station master had expected, the tall man had not fallen into his trap. John walked slowly down to meet his accomplice and both men shrugged in disappointment. 'No sign of him today then Mr. Graham.'

All of a sudden both of them froze. The bell in the box had rung out twice to signal a train was entering the Blackcraig station section. They both stared at each other in disbelief as no train could possibly be due. John and Davy turned as one to look at the little building that held the signal levers and bells. 'Oh Jesus Mr. Graham, I'm for it now. Oh, bloody Jesus, they will sack me when they find out that I held a train at the signal for no reason.' John was still staring at the box rather than the despairing young signalman.

'You don't need to worry about that, son. There is no train coming, there never was.' He took hold of Davy and swung him around, so he too looked over to his usual place of work on the opposite platform. Walking slowly down the steps from the signal box was the tall man. His long coat and hat keeping him covered as the rain and damp mist swirled all around them.

Davy had remained standing where he was while John ran towards the footbridge and over to the opposite platform. He knew he would find the visitor gone by the time he arrived at the spot they had last seen him. The station master sat down on one of the platform benches and tried to get his breath back. He stared into the distance at the railway track as it disappeared into the mist. 'You ok, Mr. Graham?' John looked up at Davy who had eventually followed him over the footbridge.

'Yes, I'm fine. I need you to do something for me, Davy.'

'Yes, Sir, so long as it's not to leave my post when a train is in our section again.' John smiled wearily as he answered.

'I want you to keep quiet about all this. I don't know what's going on but it's probably best that we say nothing, or people might think we are crazy. I'll catch the bugger eventually; I just need time to work out how to do it.' Davy stood up and started to walk back to his signal box. He stopped after a few steps and turned around.

'Mr. Graham, what if it's a spirit, you know a ghost? I mean what if the station is haunted? How the hell does he appear and then disappear?' John gave an unconvincing laugh.

'Don't be ridiculous. I'm telling you, Davy, don't go around saying that, even to your folks. They won't like it and head office might find out if people talk. There is no ghost, they don't exist. It's someone playing pranks on us and I promise you I'll get to the bottom of it, and when I do this man whoever he is will answer to me and the law.'

The evening sun was making a rare appearance as John pulled his motorbike away from the stone wall it lay propped up against. He surveyed the old machine with a feeling of shame. The stand that held it up when not in use had broken off some months before and the whole bike was starting to rust badly. A rare feeling of anger and frustration washed over him. *All these years of giving service to the railway and they simply send a letter telling me I'll need to transfer to the city or lose my job. All these bloody years of dedication and hard work and all I have is an old wreck of a motorbike. And now some idiot is trying to make a fool out of me by messing around at my station. I will get the bastard if it's the last thing I do in this job. How dare he.*

John was lost in thought as he climbed aboard the machine and revved the engine. He tried to think of wee Donnie and his wife Jean waiting for him at home as both rider and bike twisted along the narrow country lane towards the distant village of Blackcraig.

It was at the bend in the road just before Dungavel farm that the accident happened. The tall man was standing in the middle of the lane blocking the way and John only had seconds to steer the bike to the left to avoid hitting him. The brakes on the Ariel were not in the best condition but he might have made it had it not been for the potholes at the side of the road. The front wheel suddenly buckled from underneath him sending the shocked station master somersaulting through the hedge and into the adjacent field. The last thing he remembered was a figure standing over him casting its dark shadow into his soul.

It was nearly 8 o'clock in the evening before John finally made it home. Jean had put Donnie to bed so as not to frighten him when his father arrived back. Ted McLeod from Dungavel farm had found John sitting at the side of the road, his arms bruised and bleeding but luckily no serious injuries. The role of station master was still a respected post in the mid-sixties Scottish countryside and the farmer had first phoned Jean before giving her husband a lift home. Unfortunately, it looked as though the bike was a right-off.

'And you just came off because of a pothole?' Jean sensed that there was more to the story than he was letting on. She knew not to probe further though as her husband always kept things deep inside him. He hated the thought of his beloved wife having to worry about anything. John was of the old school like his father had been. A station master never deserted his post, he was a pillar of the community and he always worked to a strict timetable.

'Yes, the road near the farm is a mess. I was lucky to land in the field as it broke my fall. Thank heaven Ted came along when he did, or I might have had to walk home the last few miles. Jean finished wiping the blood away from the cut on his forehead.

'Are you sure you don't need to see a doctor? How will you get to work tomorrow, maybe Davy Sedgwick's mother will come and get you. Do you want me to give her a call?' Even though he had had a close shave Jean knew he would still go to work despite it being a Saturday and the annual Blackcraig gala weekend.

'No, you don't need to call her, I have a better idea. Pass me over the phone. I'm going to call the area manager in Dumfries and say I've had an accident. I think it's about time I came with you and Donnie to the gala at long last.' Jean looked at him in disbelief as she trailed the phone and cable over towards his seat. Times were indeed changing and if not for the better then at least this was one wee ray of light in their lives. She bent down and kissed his forehead. John looked up at her and tried to smile. There was no joy in his eyes though, how could there be? He had the tall man to deal with and this was one last fight that he did not intend to lose.

* * *

The annual Blackcraig summer gala mirrored that of most Border towns and villages in the nineteen-sixties. It was the one day of the year when everyone could let their hair down and all classes of society would mingle and enjoy themselves. Doctors would mix with farm labourers; shopkeepers would talk to schoolteachers, and for once even the local station master could be seen trying to enjoy the hustle and bustle of the big occasion. The day would start with a procession of homemade floats being pulled along by either horses or farm tractors. Each one would have a particular theme relating to village life and usually be adorned with locals in various costumes. One of the main attractions would be the village fair which would include small rides and tents advertising various pedlars of the dark and mysterious. In the afternoon competitions and games would be enjoyed until the pubs opened and the adults got down to the serious business of getting blind drunk.

John looked on as Jean placed Donnie onto the merry-go-round once more. The boy had shrieked with excitement each time the ride finished and would then plead to go back on again. The station master was enjoying the time with his family, but he was desperate to leave and go home. The locals were beginning to annoy him with their indignant false sympathy regarding the loss of the railway line. Both he and they knew why it was closing. Few of the villages used the trains anymore. The buses were more frequent and far more convenient as they ran along the high street. Some of the locals even owned their own cars and private ownership was sure to increase as people became more affluent. The reality was no one needed the railway anymore and the once-important role of the station master was a thing of the past.

The gala was now at its mid-afternoon peak as

hundreds of locals milled about the village square. John had lost sight of his family and tried to survey the scene around him in an effort to find them. Suddenly he froze as he saw the familiar fedora hat move slowly through the throng. Instantly he attempted to follow but it was as if the tall man was floating through the crowd. John either bumped into people or had to give way to young mothers pushing prams or trying to keep toddlers in check. His prey seemed to disappear just as he reached the fairground tents. John found himself standing outside one with a large colourful sign stating, *Cassandra Lylath, Soothsayer and Fortune Teller. Come in and see your future. Two shillings.*

The station master looked in frustration at the crowd, but the tall man had escaped him once more. He was just about to walk back to try and find Jean and Donnie when his gaze returned to the sign. John Graham was probably the last man in the world who would ever spend money on an old charlatan pretending to be able to read the future. And yet for reasons he could not explain his legs carried him through the drapes of the tent and inside.

The large booth was dimly lit by a multitude of burning candles that caused eery shadows to flicker across the fabric. Cassandra Lylath was nothing like what he had expected. She was probably in her late twenties, of the gipsy blood, and incredibly pretty. Dark curls tumbled down the side of her porcelain skin. She wore a tight black dress that accentuated her eye-catching curves and enormous oval silver earrings hung over the side of her face. She looked up and gave him a warm smile before shuffling the pack of cards she held in her hands. 'Good day kind sir. Take a seat and learn what your destiny holds.' John found himself sitting down almost as though it was against his will and he was in a trance. It was her, the most beautiful woman he had ever seen had him mesmerised.

'I don't wish to have my future or anything else read, Miss, erm Miss Lylath. I was looking for someone. A tall man, wearing one of those Fedora hats, I don't suppose he came in here by any chance?' The smile on her face seemed to fade slightly as though he had said something familiar, but she quickly regained her composure.

'No, I didn't see the man you talk of, but I sense that you are troubled. Lay two shillings in the palm of my hand and I may be able to help you find what you seek.' Once more John expected to stand up and leave but instead, his fingers felt inside his pocket. He awkwardly placed the two silver coins in front of the fortune teller rather than into her outstretched hand. She left them there and started to turn the cards over one by one. Suddenly as she turned the third card she stopped and abruptly stood up. The expression on her face had changed from false interest to one of fear. 'You need to leave. Take your money and go, I cannot help you.' John was completely taken aback by the woman's volte-face.

He remained seated and tried to keep calm.

'Why, what's wrong? Tell me what you see?' In normal circumstances, he would have taken her reaction as all part of the show. An act to obtain more money, get him begging for the answer for a lot more than two shillings. But, act or not, he needed to see out the charade. He had to know what she had foreseen. The fortune teller shuffled the cards back into the pack and moved over towards the exit of the tent making it obvious she wanted him to leave. She beckoned him towards the opening as her eyes looked nervously at the people milling about outside.

'Please, you must go. I have already told you that I can't help you. I'm asking you to leave, it's for your own good.' Despite her seeming reluctance, John felt that he could sense that she wanted to tell him more. Suddenly he stood up and surprised himself by taking the young woman abruptly by her shoulders.

'I'm not leaving; I'll pay you whatever it is you want. Just tell me what you saw. Please, I'm begging you, please. I have a wife and a young son who I adore. Is it anything to do with them?' Cassandra Lylath pulled herself away from his hold and edged back a few feet; her face looked troubled, but she seemed sympathetic towards the man who was now pleading for her help.

'I can't do much for you, but I will tell you what I know. But you must promise me that you will never tell anyone that I tried to help you.' John nodded his head in desperation.

'Yes, yes Miss Lylath, I'll not say a word, just tell me what I need to know.' She walked back to her chair and sat down. Her eyes seemed to sparkle as the candlelight reflected off them.

'The tall man who haunts you is the male manifestation of the Caoineag, the ancient banshee who foretells the loss of a loved one. It is she who wails for the death and he who watches for her.' The soothsayer spoke the words in a whisper as though she was frightened that they might be heard outside the tent. John listened with a mixture of horror and disbelief.

'What has this got to do with me though?' Her eyes looked sad as she replied.

'The loved one is someone that is very dear to you.'

'How do I find out who the loved one is and what can I do to change things?' The young woman stood up again and this time she meant what she said.

'You need to leave, go now before I call for help. You do not want to deal with my father or brother, go now.' The trance was broken, and the station master went to walk out of the tent. Just as he was about to leave, he turned and walked back over to the table. John took out his wallet and placed a five-pound note in front of the young woman. She gave him a worried smile before speaking her final words. 'You still have a chance. The Caoineag will offer you a forfeit that might yet save the one you love.'

* * *

Later that evening John sat dozing in front of the roaring coal fire with a full glass of whisky in his hand and the bottle at his side. He mulled over the day's events while trying desperately to place things into some kind of order that would make sense. He thought about Jean and wee Donnie safely asleep upstairs. The soothsayer had unnerved him even more than the tall man. *Was it just a coincidence that she had mentioned him? How could the young woman possibly have known that he was being haunted?* He tried to rationalise it all, but nothing seemed to fit into a logical explanation. John was not what you would consider a drinker, but he downed the glass in one gulp and then wondered why it felt so tasteless.

He woke with a start just after midnight. The fire was cold and dead in the hearth and his mouth felt dry from the whisky he had consumed. John stood shakily on his feet and staggered over to the sink. He desperately needed a long cold drink of water. As the tap gurgled the liquid out into the glass, he glanced up at the curtains that were drawn across the small kitchen window. Something was making him look, almost the same force that had directed him to walk inside the tent to see the fortune teller. He pulled the curtains apart. Standing staring at him directly on the other side was the tall man. The fedora was pulled down covering his eyes, but he could still see below where his nose should have been. The man had no skin, just blood and bones moving around as though his face was boiling in a cauldron and had melted. The station master staggered backwards and screamed before collapsing into the black hole that appeared as the floor caved in below him. Down, down he went, so fast that the sound of his shrieks could only follow like an echo from the very depths of hell.

'John, John, wake up, wake up, it's Donnie, for heaven's sake wake up.' The station master opened his eyes and tried desperately to focus. He could see Jean's face inches away from his. She was shaking him violently. 'Wake up, please get yourself together, please.' He finally realised that he had fallen asleep and had been dreaming. The fire was still burning, and the full glass of whisky was still precariously balanced at the side of his chair.

'What is it, what's wrong, Jean?'

'It's Donnie, wee Donnie, he won't move, I can hardly hear him breathing, something is badly wrong. Please John, please do something I'm scared.' His eyes had fully opened now, and he could see the tears running down his wife's face.

Within seconds he was in the bedroom holding his son in his arms. The boy was a ghastly pale colour but still breathing even if it was hardly noticeable. He could hear

Jean speaking to the operator in the hallway asking for an ambulance. The station master now knew it was no longer a coincidence. He even guessed already that the doctors would not be able to save his young child. Only he would have the power to do that. John Graham would have to find the tall man and the only person who could assist him was the soothsayer Cassandra Lylath. She would help him, she had to help him. The father would save his child even if it meant sacrificing others.

As the anxious couple waited desperately for help to arrive, four miles away the night boat train was storming through the lonely Blackcraig station. The express train did not call at the little wayside halts, so the platforms should have been empty. The oil lamps had all been extinguished for the night but the lights from the passing train windows gave a brief release from the dark night. A tall figure watched the carriages flash by underneath him as he stood on the footbridge. His eyes stared out from under the fedora, but they paid no heed to the passing train. They were firmly focused on the little village far away in the distance and the two distraught parents who cradled a silent child in their arms.

***

John ran across the car park towards the waiting

Morris Oxford that sat in one of the visitor bays at Dumfries hospital. In happier times the fact that Josh owned a car when he couldn't afford one might have irked him. Now all he felt was gratitude that the engine driver had been so helpful in coming out to collect him. Anyway, John knew that his friend worked long shifts often away from home if he was on express train work. He deserved every penny of his hard-earned money. 'Thanks, Josh, I really appreciate you doing this for me.'

'No problem John, I know it's a terrible time for you and Jean. We are all praying for wee Donnie, I'm sure the doctors will bring him back around.'

It was now Monday morning and the couple had spent the night at their boy's bedside. Jean had been surprised when John told her he would go home to get some sleep and then come back that evening to take over and allow her to do the same. He had managed to convince his wife of the practicalities of his plan even though rest was not the reason he was going back to Blackcraig. Their boy was still in a coma and for now, the doctors were unsure of the reason.

'Josh, I don't suppose you know if the fairground people are still in the village or have, they moved on yet?' His friend gave him a surprised look as he steered the car the last few yards towards John's cottage. It seemed a strange question in the circumstances, but the engine driver put it down to the situation.

'They were still on the village green when I passed by earlier on the way to get you. I could see them starting to take down the tents and packing up. They'll be off to the next village gala no doubt. Somewhere else they can squeeze more money out of the locals.'

John waited inside the house to make sure the car was out of sight before he walked back through the door and hurried towards the village centre. It was only 9 am and the dew was still on the damp grass waiting for the temperature to rise. It was that time of the morning when the day is still young, and the earth has a clean slate that only the human race can ruin.

The station master could see that the gipsy menfolk were already up and busying themselves with taking down the booths and fairground rides. He walked over towards one of the burly men, the muscles of his uncovered torso bathed in sweat as he toiled in the early morning sun. 'Good day to you. I wonder if you could help me. I'm looking for the caravan that Miss Cassandra Lylath the fortune teller stays in?' The man stopped what he was doing and turned to face the station master. His expression was both unfriendly and mocking.

'What business you got with Miss Cassandra then?' John felt his face redden as he tried to think of an answer. He regretted the words he spoke almost the second they left his mouth. The station master had been so used to being respected all his life but now he felt threatened. His world of rigid train timetables and order was disintegrating around him.

'If you don't mind, that is none of your business. Now do you know what caravan Miss Cassandra is in or should I ask someone who does?' The man dropped the mallet he was holding in his hand and moved his face within inches of the beleaguered station master. The veins in his neck bulged while his bloodshot eyes stared unblinking into those of his potential victim.

'Say one more word and I'll rip ya fuckin head of ya doity stinkin gorger.' John realised he was in trouble and started to back away. Suddenly he felt a hand on his shoulder and fully expecting to take a punch in the mouth he spun around with his arm covering his face. Cassandra Lylath stood in front of him. The black curls of her hair cascading down over the smooth skin of her bare shoulders.

'Leave him be, Menowin. It's ok, I'll speak with him.' The large man gave the station master a disdainful look and then swept his head back and laughed mockingly.

'Ok, Risa, if that's what you want. The stinkin gorger is all yours.' The girl started to walk toward one of the caravans. Every one of the gipsy men had stopped working to watch the fracas. John could feel the eyes of suspicion and dislike on him as he followed in the footsteps of the beautiful Risa.

She closed the door of the caravan and told him to sit

down before taking a seat on the opposite side of a small table that separated them. The inside was decorated with a myriad of flowered throws and cushions. Gold-plated rails adorned shelves that seemed to cover every inch of available space. A multitude of exotic ornaments standing on each one. A large double bed with gloriously colourful woven blankets took up most of the top half of the caravan. Lit candles were dotted around shedding a low light that reflected off the heavily curtained windows. John felt overawed as he looked at the young woman. He was desperate to ask for her help, but the words he wanted to say would not come out. 'Why do they call you Risa, I thought your name was Cassandra?' She smiled and her deep blue eyes twinkled.

'My real name is Risa. The other one is just for you locals to make me sound exotic. I need to earn a living, don't I?' Suddenly her expression changed and her face hardened.

'I know why you are here, John Graham.' The station master should have been taken aback by the fact she knew his name, but little would surprise him now.

'The only way you can save your boy is to do exactly as I tell you. You must understand that I'm taking a massive risk even speaking to you. I do so only because you have a child and I know what that means.' For the first time, John could sense a vulnerability in the young woman. He knew he must not ask but sensed that she too had faced the trauma of losing a loved one. It was only as she spoke the words that he noticed the photograph of a very young boy on one of the shelves. Small candles burned beside the frame and John wondered if they held the reason why she was breaking the gipsy tradition and allowing a gorger into her home.

'Yes, yes, please Risa, I'll listen to anything, anything. Please just tell me what it is I must do.' She held her hand up to stop him from talking any further.

'Only the Watcher can tell you what to do. He is the eyes of The Caoineag, she who forever mourns death. The Watcher must feed the misery of the banshee. Find him and do what he asks of you and your boy may yet live.' John's eyes were watering now, the emotion was starting to overwhelm him. He would save wee Donnie no matter what was required.

'This Watcher you speak off, how do I find him? Is he the tall man who has been following me? Every time I see him, he disappears.' She lifted a pack of cards that lay on the table in front of her and dealt the first three onto the table before him. Her eyes then lifted to look at John, he could see the fear and sadness in them.

'Duncarron, it spells the name Duncarron. Does that mean anything to you?' She could tell by his reaction that he recognised the place she had mentioned.

'Yes, yes, it's the name of an isolated railway tunnel a mile or so further on from my station at Blackcraig. Duncarron tunnel on the Port Line, is that where I'll find him?' She folded the cards away and stood up making it obvious that the talk was over.

'The Caoineag will always have a place she can stay to wail and bring misery. She will only move once The Watcher has brought her a new death to mourn.'

'So, that is the place I'll find them?' She opened the door and spoke in a loud unfriendly tone as if she wanted those outside to hear what she said.

'I cannot help you; I have told you all I know, now go. Go before I set Menowin on you again.' John reluctantly stood up and walked over to the door but just as he was about to step outside, he heard Risa whisper to him in a soft sad tone. 'John Graham, you must go to this Duncarron place but be aware there will be a price to pay for your boy's life and it will not come easy for you.' With those words, she slammed the door shut as he stepped outside. The gipsy menfolk continued to stare at him until he was finally out of sight.

***

Despite the weather being dry and the sun attempting to break through the clouds, John struggled to make progress across the boggy heather and grass. It was now almost midday and even though his limbs ached, and his feet were soaking, he pressed on. A mile or so in the distance he could just make out the familiar sight of the railway embankment that seemed to disappear into the hillside. This was the point where the line entered the three-quarter mile long Duncarron tunnel. He had walked through it many times previously in his role as a permanent way inspector before his promotion to station master. It was a bleak and inaccessible place that would only be visited on foot if absolutely necessary.

John had borrowed old Tam McCready's bicycle from next door without asking. His neighbour had not been in when he hammered on the door. There was no time for formalities, John knew he had to act fast if he was to save his beloved boy. The 5-mile ride along the little road through the hills had not been a problem, it was the last mile of hiking across the lonely bleak moor that had slowed him up. There was no track to the tunnel as it stood high and isolated on the side of a steep hill. Each step had seen his black work shoes sink deeper into the wet peaty bog. It took the station master almost a further hour to finally reach the eastern portal of the impressive Victorian engineering feat. The entrance was hidden down a steep brick-lined cutting that dripped with water seeping in from the hillside.

John inched carefully down towards the track. Any accident now could prove to be disastrous for both him and the life of his son. The station master had tried to switch his logical thought processes off. He desperately hoped that the tale the fortune teller had told him was true. It was the only way that he could feel he was back in control of his destiny. He needed something to cling to, something that would allow him to save his boy. He had no fear of meeting the Caoineag or anyone else. It was his only hope. If he entered the tunnel and found it empty, then there was nothing further that he could do. At least the story of the tall man gave him something to hang on to. It gave him a timetable he could work with.

John at last edged down the remaining few feet and onto the track. He instinctively took out his railway watch from the top pocket of his jacket and checked the time. 13:16, he still had 45 minutes until the next train came through. Plenty of time to explore inside and see if the young woman spoke the truth. Even if the train came while he was in the tunnel then John knew that he could stand safely in one of the recesses. They had been built into the wall at intervals to aid any railway staff involved in engineering work.

He chastened himself for not having the foresight to bring a torch. Only a few hundred yards beyond the portal it was becoming difficult to see. The daylight still shone from the opening, but it was soon being swallowed up with each step he took into the ominous black cavern. Something made him turn around to look back at the tunnel mouth. A figure was standing watching him. He recognised her immediately, it was Cassandra Lylath or Risa as she was known. John now knew that the tale of the banshee must be true. There could be no other explanation as to how the young woman had gotten here. He turned back around and continued his journey into the depths but now with a real sense of purpose. It was becoming so dark that the only way he could move forward was to keep close to one of the rails as it threaded its way towards the western exit of the tunnel.

At first, the only sound he could hear was the crunch of his feet on the stone ballast and the dripping of water from the roof of the cavern. And then it came, drifting towards him with each step. Almost like the sound of a dying animal suffering in agony when it realises that the end is here. A bitter low mourning wail, a sad whimper but getting closer and now almost upon him.

His eyes had started to adjust to the dark and he could just make out the faint outline of the old woman. He took the final few steps and edged up beside her. She was so wasted and decrepit that her bones seemed to protrude from the torn rags that barely covered her ancient body. John could just about see the oval of her toothless mouth as it opened to let the continuous mourn of grief escape into the damp air. She lay propped up against the wet rock of the tunnel wall. 'Old woman, I was told you could help me save my son.' Suddenly she stopped wailing and John could see her wizened old skull start to move in his direction. It was almost as if she was trying to smile. But it was not him she was looking at. Her head had turned to look further down into the darkness at what was approaching. John could clearly make out the figure of The Watcher floating towards him. A pale glow that could only emanate from hell itself seemed to shroud his tall figure. The hat was gone, and his face spoke only of death.

'John Graham, do not say a word until it speaks to you. You will only have to answer one question. This is your last chance to save your son.' The station master did not look at Cassandra Lylath who had suddenly appeared beside him. He focused intently on the apparition that floated in front of him directly beside the now silent old hag. The words it spoke were as cold and lifeless as death itself.

'Do you John Graham accept the role of The Watcher? Will you let your soul float in eternity to free mine?' The station master did not understand, but he was afraid to speak in case he said the wrong thing for his dying child. He could see the shadow of the young woman beside him and her words now floated into his brain without her opening her mouth.

You must forfeit your life to save your son. But there is a heavier price to pay than just death. For the only way The Watcher can finally rest in peace is to pass on the role as the Caoineag can never stop mourning. For she is even more cursed than he. You will live in death forever until you too can find someone who will take your place to save a loved one. The Watcher only gets one chance, after that he too becomes a

Caoineag with no escape from an eternity of mourning.

And now the station master finally understood. The only way to save young Donnie was for him to free The Watcher and take his place. He looked at the apparition and could see it was starting to fade already. He had to answer now before it was too late. John Graham almost shouted the words in desperation, 'I agree, I will accept if it means my boy will live.' The second he finished speaking the words he was once again alone in the tunnel. John looked back at the light shining through the eastern portal. He felt completely normal and alive. *Am I going insane, has all this been in my imagination?*

John started to walk back the way he had come. It was time to get back to Dumfries hospital and find out what was happening. Somehow, he felt more hopeful, *maybe some of what the soothsayer had told him might be true.* The station master was so lost in his thoughts that he committed the cardinal sin that would have had his father and grandfather turning in their grave. No man of the railway in his position would ever fail to remember the importance of the train timetable. It was everything the station master stood for, without that what was the point?

The driver of the early afternoon Dumfries train had no idea that they had hit a man in Duncarron tunnel until they arrived at Blackcraig station a mile or so away. It was old Blacky the fireman who first saw the blood on the front of the engine. The young signalman had spotted it as he looked out the window of his signal box and shouted down to the engine crew. At first, they assumed it was a deer or maybe a sheep they had hit. It wasn't until a few days later that a search party found the decapitated and lifeless body of John Graham laying a few hundred yards inside Duncarron tunnel.

* * *

Jean smiled as she watched the two boys chase each other around the little garden of the cottage. Donnie was now in his first year at primary school and his best friend Bobby McPake was rarely away from his side. Her son's recovery from sudden illness a few years back had been remarkable and the one thing that had gotten her through the terrible loss of her husband, John. She mused on the irony that her son's best friend was the grandchild of the man who had unwittingly been involved in the death of her boy's father. She held no grudge though. The whole thing had been a tragic accident.

The verdict had been suicide and Jean had finally come to accept that her husband's death had probably been inevitable. In the months before he had taken his own life, she had noticed how her normally level-headed partner had been acting strangely. The warning sign had been there the morning he told her he was going home instead of staying with their child at the hospital. Josh and other railway colleagues had also told her he had been different in the months up to his suicide. The final piece of the jigsaw had come from the young signalman at Blackcraig, Davy Sedgwick. He had told Jean of harrowing tales regarding John claiming to see invisible passengers, hearing none-existent bells ringing, and worse of all, telling him to leave his post when a train was in the station.

Jean went into the kitchen to make the boys some lunch. As she prepared their sandwiches, she glanced through the window at old Josh who sat on the garden wall smiling. He adored his grandson Bobby and would regularly walk over with him to see Donnie. Josh had left the railway after the accident; he had been near retirement age anyway. Now it no longer mattered, the railway was already being torn up having closed six months previously. All those years of serving the community were being obliterated along with the many local jobs that came with it.

Jean had spoken to Josh's wife Helen about her concerns. The old train driver had been an incredible support to the Grahams since the death of John. He was always over either repairing the house, doing the garden or helping with the boys. Maybe a lot of it was guilt on Josh's part but Jean appreciated his help as she was now a single mother. Lately, though Josh had been acting differently. He no longer seemed carefree and in control. He looked a lot older than his 62 years, she wondered if the hard life on the railway had finally taken its toll on him.

Josh stood up and followed the two children as they ran excitedly to the garden wall. A long row of caravans pulled by horses and tractors was moving slowly along the road towards the village green. Walking beside one of the vans was a striking young woman with long black curls cascading down over her bare shoulders. 'Grandpa, it's the shows, it's the shows. Can we go to the village gala this weekend, please grandpa, please?' The two boys jumped around and hugged each other with excitement.

The old man smiled as he watched the cavalcade roll past but suddenly his face stiffened. His eyes were drawn to the distant hills that overlooked the edge of the village. In a field on the other side of the road, a tall figure wearing a fedora hat was standing staring at the cottage. The tall man was back once more. Josh squinted his eyes to try and focus better. *It's him again. Who the hell is he and why does he keep watching me from afar?*

***

For now, I know who I am, and what I am. You will know me as The Watcher; I bring death for her to mourn. I am the servant to the Caoineag, and I will always be damned to an eternity of living death unless I make the right choice. I have but one chance to return my body to the ground and give up my soul. I have chosen who might die and who must die and become The Watcher if they are to save the one, they love. I feel no guilt in choosing the man who was responsible for my death. I have no remorse that his beloved grandchild will be at risk. I will do whatever is required to be free of this half-life. I know he will answer the question correctly and take my place. Josh will do the right thing, as I did, and those who suffered before me.

<u>You</u>

It's your eyes that take me into your soul.
Like a bottomless valley pulling me deep inside.
They may glisten like the still water of a lake in the sun
They may dim when the world closes in
I can read your mind by the depth in your eyes
I see my image reflecting as our spirits collide
Like a still photograph that captured eternity
I will forever remain bound by the dream
Of seeing all that I ever desired to see.

In Memory of the True Rab Gifford

'Right, what are you guys having? It's my round.' Big Rab jumped up from the table as he spoke the words. It was said more in the tone of an order rather than a request. Wee Tony was the first to break rank. He looked at the large clock behind the bar and then nervously placed his hand around his still half-full pint glass.

'Not me, Rab, I told the missus I'd be home by eight.' The other drinkers sat around the large oval table now split into their usual ranks. Soapy and Stevie Boy grabbed the lifeline thrown to them by Wee Tony and also declined the offer of another beer. This left just Paul and Joe Slash to remain in the round. Even these two hardened drinkers would eventually stagger out of The Clachan around ten o'clock. Rab would be with them but everyone knew that he would then end up on his own in The Wee Dookit on Cross Street until closing time around midnight.

'Fuckin poofs. You lot scared of your women then? C'mon, wan mer round and then we'll call it a night.' The usual scenario would then play out as the potential early leavers were shamed into having another beer. This would no doubt be followed by a row from the missus when they arrived home late, just the way the big man had predicted.

Rab staggered up to the bar. He felt a bit shaky on his feet. This was unusual for him as he was renowned in the Glasgow Southside for being able to handle his drink. The accolade did not necessarily mean he would behave with the booze. It just meant he could drink gallons of the stuff until he eventually stumbled back to his flat and slept it off.

The Clachan was busy now with the young team starting to filter in as the evening wore on. It would annoy Rab if one of the bar staff did not serve him right away. He waited for a few minutes until it was his turn but just as he was about to order Clinchy the barman went to serve a young girl first. 'Clinchy, you tryin to be fuckin smart? Whit's the chances of getting served a fuckin drink in this dump.' The barman looked nervously at the tall red-faced man glowering at him. The girl had been waiting longer than Rab, but he knew the big man could be very volatile when drunk.

'Sorry, Rab mate. I'll get yours next, six lagers wasn't it?'

'Aye, if ye can fucking do your job ya fucking dick.' The barman stopped serving the girl and shook his head at Rab.

'That's oot of order big man, there are female customers in here and I don't like your language or being threatened.'

Rab got ready to spout more vitriol but the potential flash point was quickly brought under control by the elderly man who was standing behind him. Mad Jack was so-called because there had been tales that he had once murdered someone and got away with it. Either way, whether true or not, he was not someone to be messed with despite being well into his sixties. His reputation meant that he was respected by all in the pub. He calmed both Rab and the barman down before helping him carry the six pints back to the table.

'You guys want to keep this lunatic under control.' He said the words in a friendly tone and Rab smiled and thanked him.' Mad Jack walked back to the bar to get his order. Clinchy poured him a pint of Guinness without needing to ask what he wanted.' Sorry, Jack. It's that Rab, he is a pain in the arse once he gets drunk.' Mad Jack nodded in agreement.

'You said it Clinchy. One day someone will take that prick out. He's got it coming to him.'

***

Wee Tony jumped out of the van and waved to the driver as it sped off through the rush hour traffic. He was desperate for a beer having spent all day breathing in the dust as they worked on the latest tenement renovation. He walked towards the entrance of The Clachan with the two voices in his head doing battle.

Big Rab will be in there for sure and that'll be you in for another long drinking session.

No, he won't and even if he is, I can just have two pints

and get up the road for six o'clock, keep her happy.

Don't talk fucking daft man, Big Rab will insist you stay, and you're too scared to say no.

Yes, maybe you're right. I should just go home, have a drink with the missus instead.

That's the way to do it, wee man. Go home, see the wife, and keep clear of that nutjob. Well done.

Wee Tony pushed the door of the pub open and walked inside. He tried not to show the relief he felt when the gang's usual table held just Stevie Boy and Paul.

'You guys want a beer?' It was customary for any newcomer walking into the boozer to offer his mates a drink even if they already had one. The guy asking would always hope they would say no. The guys seated would usually say yes unless they had only taken a small sip out of their current pint. Tony could see that they had only taken two mouthfuls and he might get away with having to buy an expensive round.

'Och, go on then. Lager for me.' Paul's words were quickly echoed by Stevie Boy.

A few minutes later Tony was back at the table precariously placing the three pints he held in his arms onto the table. 'You guys ok? How're things ?' He did not want to ask straight away if Big Rab was around in case he made it too obvious that he was hoping he wouldn't be.

'You alright, wee man? You hear about that fucking

nutter Rab last night?' Tony now dropped all pretence and looked towards his two mates with anticipation.

'No, go on, tell me. What's the big man been up to now?' Stevie Boy sat back making it obvious that Paul was the man with the information. Paul straightened up in his chair as though he was about to give a momentous speech of the utmost importance.

'Well we were all here last night, Big Rab was with us.' Wee Tony interrupted him to protest.

'I fucking know that; I was here with you guys as well.' Paul gave him a puzzled look.

'Were you? Sorry, Tony. Are you sure?' Stevie Boy laughed and jumped in.

'Yes, for fuck sake Paul, you were talking to him, of course, he was here ya daft eejit. You want tae stay off the beer. Anyway, shut the fuck up arguing you two and tell him the story.' Paul took a large drink from one of his two pints and continued.

'Well, we were all here last night in The Clachan. Oh yes, I told you that bit. Yes, so, me and Joe Slash left this place at about eleven with Big Rab. Maybe about an hour after all you lightweights went home. Me and Joe were fucking minging with the drink but Big Rab talked us into going for a final beer in The Wee Dookit.' Tony listened intently. Even though he was considered to be one of Rab's mates he hoped the big man had maybe got what was coming to him.

It would make life in the pub easier for all of them.

'Yes, go on then. What happened?' Paul coughed before continuing. Years of smoking cigarettes and joints had played havoc with his lungs.

'Am trying tae fucking tell ye. Will you shut up and let me speak.' Wee Tony nodded while taking a gulp from his pint.

'Well, we get into The Wee Dookit and it must have been later than we thought. The barman, Shug, you know him, that prick who always wears a white shirt and thinks he's God's gift to the women. Anyway, he tells Rab that it's last orders and the big man goes, *well give us six pints and three whiskies then*. Shug tells him there is not enough time for us to drink all that and we can have three pints, that's all. So Big Rab says nothing and then when Shug places the beer on the counter for him, he drinks one of the pints in a single go. He then does the same with the second pint. I mean, cheeky bastard drinks both mine and Joe's beer. But, that's not all. Guess what the fucking nutjob does with the third beer?'

'Go on, what does he do? Don't tell me he drinks that in a one-go as well.' Paul sits back and takes another slow gulp from his glass before delivering the dramatic punchline.

'Fuckin nutjob only goes and grabs Shug by the collar of his white shirt and pours the third pint over his head.' Stevie Boy lets out a belly laugh even though he has now heard the story a few times. Even Wee Tony is forced to relax and laugh before he makes a comment.

'Jeez, what did Shug do? I can't see him taking that lightly, him being the manager.' Paul leans forward with dramatic purpose, there is a second punchline coming.

'Shug went fucking mental; his white shirt was ruined. Him and that other barman Leapy called the cops but before they arrived Big Rab hurled the empty glass across the bar. It smashed Leapy a cracker right on the side of his big ugly face. There was pandemonium, me and Joe Slash got the hell out of it before the Feds arrived. No one has heard anything from Rab since last night. Big man might even be in the jail.'

Wee Tony sat back to ponder the sensational story. He tried hard not to smile and show his pleasure at the news. There could be little doubt that Big Rab had gone over the top this time. Pouring a pint over the manager's head was bad enough but hurling a glass at one of the staff was a step too far. Tony just wished all this had happened in The Clachan instead of The Wee Dookit. It would have meant Big Rab was barred for life and they could all drink in peace.

Suddenly Paul leaned forward as though he was about to deliver even more startling news. Wee Tony readied himself in anticipation as Paul spoke.

'Did any of you see the Celtic game at the weekend? That wis never a sending aff. Fuckin ref must have been a blue nose.'

* * *

Rab moved his face to within a few inches of the bathroom mirror. He tried to remember what had happened the previous evening but only got as far as being in The Clachan. Even he could see that drinking was starting to take its toll on him. In the past, he would be able to recount every move he made but in recent months his memory had started to forget to remind him what he had been up to the night before. For the first time in his life, he started to contemplate the fact that he looked older than his 34 years. The guys in the boozer were all around his age and had mostly settled down. They were either married with kids or at least had a permanent partner. Ok, Joe Slash was still single, but the gang would have put that down to him being both ugly and a man who liked his booze too much.

The big man's introspection was quickly over as he smiled and decided to pull himself together. *Rab, you're still a handsome bastard compared to those eejits in the pub. I can stop drinking whenever I want. It's just that I don't want to right now.*

There could be little doubt that Rab was indeed the sort of man that most women desired. Tall, rugged, jet-black hair, a smart but casual dress sense, and of course edgy and dangerous to be with. Over the years he had slept with countless women but the only one he had ever really cared for was Tracy. Four years younger than him she was still a stunning-looking woman. Rab was the envy of everyone in The Clachan, most wondered why she stuck with him when his true love was really alcohol. And yet, every guy probably wanted to be him, the man who had Tracy at his beck and call. The man who lived life to the full. But recently things had started to change. Now she had turned thirty Tracy was beginning to question her relationship with Big Rab. She hoped he would change and settle down, but his endless promises were starting to sound hollow and meaningless. His charm and charisma were becoming clouded by alcohol.

Rab was startled to hear the doorbell of his flat ring. *Who would call at nine in the morning?* He had already texted Tree Boy to say he was not up for labouring today and Tracy didn't finish her shift at the hospital until ten. Anyway, she would usually go back to her flat to sleep and then call him in the afternoon if she was coming over. He unlocked the door and pulled it open. Two middle-aged men stood in the doorway. One wearing a scruffy old suit, the other covered by a long raincoat.

'Robert Gifford?' Rab knew straight away that it was the police. It was not the first time that he had had a run-in with the law. He could smell them coming.

'Aye, it says that on the fucking door plate. They don't call you Sherlock Holmes for nothing.' The Old Suit eyed him up with a resigned impatience.

'Mr Gifford. We need to speak to you about an assault last night at The Wee Dookit public bar on Cross Street. Now you can either be a smart arse and we will simply take you to the station or you can try to be a clever little boy and invite us in to talk. You call it, it's your shout tough guy.' A vague memory was edging back into Rab's still drink-addled brain. He could see a glass being thrown and a barman with blood running down the side of his face. It was time to back down, damage limitation was the name of the game now.

'No problem officer, you better come in. Can I get you guys a tea or a coffee?'

Fifteen minutes later a very relieved Rab was opening the door of his flat to let the two detectives out. The fact that Leapy had only minor cuts and did not want to press charges was not lost on him. He knew that Shug the manager would not want to make an enemy of the big man but the cops coming round to see him was a warning for the future.

'Thanks, guys, I appreciate the visit and can only apologise, it's so unlike me to do something like that. I'll nip up to The Dookit later on and say sorry to the guys.' The Old Suit stopped in his tracks and turned around.

'Listen, son, you're not getting this, are you? First of all, you're barred from The Wee Dookit for life. Shug told me to pass that message on. Secondly, we are watching you. Maybe you got away with it this time big fella but eventually, you'll screw up again and when you do, we will be ready for you. Seen it all before, big shot smart guy who can't hold his drink ends up in the pokey.' Rab dropped all pretence of being friendly and gave his parting shot before slamming the door closed.

'Aye right, am fucking pishing ma self, big man. Have a nice day boys. Enjoy helping old ladies to cross the street.'

Outside on the landing the old suit turned to the raincoat and laughed. 'That big prick thinks he is so clever. I'll bet you a tenner I get him in the end. Cardboard gangsters like Rab Gifford are so fucking stupid that they walk into the trap with their arms outstretched.' Raincoat nodded in agreement before replying.

'Aye, your right boss. He's one to watch, got a mouth on him the size of his heid.'

Rab walked back into his living room and sat down with a heavy heart. His head still hurt from the boozing the night before and the police visit had unnerved him. For a few seconds, a feeling of vulnerability washed over him. *Maybe I need to cool it, keep out the pub for a while. Maybe try and get things back on track with Trace. Yes, I could buy a ring, surprise her.*

He stood up and walked to the kitchen to get a coffee but only got as far as the cabinet beside the door of the living room. A few minutes later he had settled back into his favourite comfy chair. A glass in his hand and a three-quarter full bottle of cheap vodka at his side. *Just a couple of wee shorts to take the edge off this fucking headache.*

It was mid-afternoon when Rab awoke bewildered and disorientated. The glass had fallen to the floor and the bottle was empty. He stared at it in disbelief, *how the fuck did I manage to drink all that?* His confusion was made even more acute by the noises floating around in his head. A mobile phone was ringing in the bedroom and he knew it would be Tracy telling him she was on her way over. But it was the other noise that was unnerving him. It was the sound of running water. He tried to focus his addled brain to work out what was happening. *Oh, Fuck, have I left the taps on while I was drunk, Jeez the place might be flooded.* It was then that it dawned on him that the sound was coming from the shower. He lifted his frame out of the chair and staggered into the hall. The bathroom door was slightly ajar, and steam was escaping out and floating up towards the ceiling. The walls were damp with condensation as though the shower had been running for hours. Rab pushed the door open and was hit by a wall of hot steam. He stood transfixed looking at the Perspex shower screen. A naked male figure was inside with its back to him. He was soaping himself down and whistling away as though the unfolding scenario was the most natural thing in the world. Rab edged slowly up to the screen just as the person turned to face him. The man was him. It was his absolute double who was in the shower. Rab staggered back in shock and suddenly his feet slipped from under him on the shiny wet bathroom floor. He went crashing to the ground as his head smacked off the damp tiles.

He opened his eyes and looked up at the figure of Tracy who was shaking him violently. 'For God's sake, what a bloody mess to be in at two in the afternoon. Get up off the floor you idiot.'

It was an unusually sheepish Rab who sat on the couch in the living room of his flat. His hands were shaking as he tried to sip the hot coffee the irate Tracy had made him. He had never seen her so angry. She refused to listen to his confused lies any longer. He tried to explain what had happened, but she knew the truth. He was drunk, he was always drunk. When she finally calmed down, she gave him an ultimatum. Tracy had heard about the confrontation in the Wee Dookit. Even her parents and friends knew what had happened, he was the talk of the Southside. Either he give up drinking or she was finished with him for good. No more last chances.

'I will doll, that's me aff it. Never again, am done with it.' Tracy gave him a rueful smile as she picked up her handbag to leave. 'Trace don't go, am really sorry darlin. Please stay, I promise I won't drink ever again.' She looked at him with tears forming in her eyes and then bent down and gave him an affectionate kiss on the forehead.

'I'm going Rab. Tree Boy called me at work and said you had let him down again. Said to tell you he needs someone more reliable as he has too much work on. Told me to tell you not to bother going back.'

'Oh right. Is the wee fucker too frightened to say it to ma face then? He can go fuck himself for all I care. Let's see how he gets on pruning trees without me doing all the graft for him.' Tracy held up her hand with impatience. She had heard it all before.

'That's the problem Rab. He is scared of you. Can't you see it, everyone is scared of you. Once you get a drink, you're horrible. No one likes an obnoxious boring drunk.' Rab felt the anger rising in his veins. He had never heard Tracy be so blunt with him before.

'Och well fuck you then. Fuck the lot of you.' As soon as he spoke the words, he regretted them. Without replying she turned and walked towards the door and out into the landing. 'Trace, Trace, I didn't mean that. I'll stop boozing; we can get married. Look, please, I'm sorry. I love you darlin, come on, wan mer chance.' She gave him a final rueful look before leaving.

'Aye right, Rab. I wish I could believe you but how many times have you said the same thing? I'm sorry but I just can't take this crap anymore. Look after yourself and if I'm still around when you come to your senses and stop drinking then maybe you can call me.'

Rab sat in his chair feeling sorry for himself. He knew Tracey was right and that it was time for him to screw the nut and stop drinking. The problem was he had started on one of his usual two to three-day benders and he was only halfway through it. *Once this one was over that would be him finished with drinking for good. He meant it this time.* He walked into the kitchen and checked the cupboards for alcohol. There was nothing left. Fifteen minutes later Rab was on his way to the off licence. *Just one bottle of vodka, just the one to take the edge off and then I'll get my life sorted out.*

* * *

Rab could see daylight penetrating through the drawn curtains of his bedroom. He knew he had been on a bender and this was him coming through on the other side, but he had no idea how long he had been out of it. He could smell the stench of alcohol and sweat as he looked down at his still-fully clothed body. It was time to get back into the real world and sort his problems out. This was it, this time he meant business.

A few hours later Big Rab stood in front of the mirror combing his hair. He looked better after a shower but there was no hiding the dark circles under his bloodshot eyes. He had been amazed to find that two days had passed since Tracy had stormed out of his flat. There were some missed messages on his phone but most of them had been from his friends or parents. The fact that the most important person in his life had not called made him realise just how much he had screwed up this time. Three empty vodka bottles and a coffee table littered with the remnants of various joints added to his sense of guilt and shame. Rab could only surmise that he had got so wasted that he'd fallen asleep for most of the time. The concern was, he could remember nothing since Tracy had left.

Rab jumped with surprise as he heard his mobile ring out from the bedroom. It took him a while before he located it laying on the floor underneath the bedside cabinet. Beside it was an empty half bottle of whisky. He could see that it was Tracy ringing and he desperately tried to answer but the phone died almost immediately. The next few minutes were spent in a panic while he tried to find his charger. Eventually, the phone kicked back into life but before he could call Tracy back a message pinged up. *Hi Gorgeous. I just love the new you. Maybe it won't last but I so hope it does. You are so different when you stay off the drink. I'm going to work now so won't be able to take any calls. See you tonight at The Clachan. Can't wait to go to the cinema, popcorn and hotdogs are on me. xx*

To say that the big man was confused would be an understatement. Not only did he have no idea what Tracy was talking about he also could not work out how he had drunk so much. He could only recall having bought one bottle of vodka and yet he had found three empty ones. Even more weird was the half bottle of whiskey in his bedroom. *He never touched the stuff, where the hell had that come from?* There was only one thing left to do. Make his return to The Clachan and have a few beers. That would freshen him up for when Tracy finished work and he could find out what the hell was going on.

Rab took one last look in the mirror. He thought he looked good, blue open-neck shirt, tight jeans, expensive white trainers and his best Italian Jacket. The sleep had done him good. He felt hungry, *maybe he would get some grub at The Clachan. Get a few beers down first. Stay sober and have a decent meal.* As he turned to close the door to his flat, he could hear someone coming up the stairs of the close. The big man stood transfixed as the figure simply headed towards him and then brushed him aside before walking through the still-open door of his apartment. It took a few moments for Rab to take in the fact that he was watching an image of himself, be it a healthier looking one. He finally took hold of his senses and charged after the figure. 'Who the fucking hell are you and what the fuck are you doing in my flat?' The man stopped and turned around, a big smile on his face.

'What are you talking about Rab? It's me, well it's you is maybe what I should say. Wow, that Tracy of ours is one hot little thing in bed. We are so lucky to have her.' Rab had stopped listening, he had his eyes tightly shut and was throwing angry uncoordinated punches in the direction of the figure. Within seconds he was out of breath and a sharp pain was pumping through his chest. He bent down and held his sides before opening his eyes. Beads of sweat were running down his face. The hall was empty. Rab wiped his forehead with his hand and walked back to the door. *I need a fucking drink.*

** * ***

It only dawned on Big Rab that it was Thursday evening when he walked into the Clachan. For most pub-going Glaswegians, the weekend now extended to three days rather than the traditional two. All of the gang were already seated at the table. Soapy, Stevie Boy, Wee Tony, Paul, and Joe Slash. Rab grunted a hello before scanning the pints on the table. 'I take it you fuckers are wanting a beer?' Unusually it was Wee Tony who stood up and answered. He was smiling and seemed more relaxed than usual, especially if Big Rab had just turned up.

'No, take a seat, Rab, you spent enough buying us all drink last night. I'll get you one. Are you looking forward to the film tonight? I take it you're still on the fresh orange and lemonade?' Rab stared at him incredulously before stuttering an angry reply.

'What the fuck are you on about Tony? You trying to wind me up? I'll take ye fucking outside and let you play with your fucking teeth ya wee prick.' The gang all looked at him in shock. It was dawning on Rab that something weird was going on, but he had no idea what it was. He could feel the eyes of the whole pub on him wondering if the madman was going to kick off again. The attack on the barman at The Wee Dookit some days back was still fresh in people's minds. Rab suddenly felt cornered and self-conscious. 'Aww fuck this and fuck you lot.' He turned around and stormed out of the pub leaving his bemused friends to look at each other with a mixture of surprise and confusion.

Two hours later Rab was sitting on a stool at the bar in The Caledonian. He rarely frequented the pub on Cregnathan Road as it was a mile or so from his flat, but he needed to get away from those who knew him well. A few of the locals nodded but most kept their distance, his reputation stretched across the Southside. The only explanation he could think of for the strange things happening was that he had been so drunk he had actually been to the Clachan yesterday and not remembered. But what about the message from Tracy and why was he imagining seeing his doppelganger? *It's the booze, I know it's the fucking booze. I need to get off this stuff. That's it, am finished with the drink for good.*

Rab was lost in his thoughts as he emptied his sixth pint and then nodded to the barman for another. He felt a tap on his shoulder and turned around to see Joe Slash standing there. 'Hi Rab, thought I might find you in here.

One of the only pubs left in Glasgow that you're not barred from.' Joe said the words with a grin on his face. He had never been the brightest candle in the night but Rab liked him. He was probably the only one in the gang who could get away with a comment like that.

'Ok, Slash old boy. Get you a pint?'

Rab sat for the next hour and listened in stunned amazement while Joe talked him through what had happened the day before. Apparently, Rab had turned up in The Clachan and roundly apologised to each and every one of them for his behaviour the night before. Not only that he had bought three rounds for them while he sipped a fresh orange and lemonade. Tracy had then arrived looking gorgeous and both she and Rab had gone out to one of the local restaurants for dinner. Rab had returned later and bought a final round for Slash and Paul before walking Tracy home. Everyone had been impressed with the new Rab and most of all Tracy. He had been telling everyone that they were off to see the new James Bond movie on Thursday evening and that he would not be in the pub for a while as he was off the booze. That was why they had all been so surprised to see him.

The two friends continued drinking until closing time. It suddenly dawned on Rab that he had not checked his phone for hours. He was shocked to see that it was blank. Not a single call or text from Tracy. Suddenly anger fuelled by alcohol welled up inside him. He stood up abruptly and grabbed his jacket. Joe drunkenly tried to take hold of his arm as he made to leave. 'Hey big man were you gawn, still time for wan mer and it's your fucking round.' Rab nearly toppled over as he tried to multi-task by walking in one direction while being pulled in the other. He roughly pushed Slash back sending him tumbling off his bar stool. Joe got shakily back to his feet and should have left it there, but booze was also clouding his senses.

'Fuck ye playin at ya dick. Ye could've broken ma back da'in that. Whit the fuck is up with…'

Unfortunately, Joe did not get to the end of the sentence as Rab viciously headbutted him sending the stunned victim hurtling back to the ground. Blood spurted out of his nose as the rest of the bar looked on in shocked disbelief.

The big man walked unsteadily along Victoria Road trying unsuccessfully to hail a taxi. It was a few miles to Tracy's flat and he knew he would struggle to make it. He felt tired, drunk, and confused. To make matters worse his phone was once again out of charge. He knew she would be asleep by now and would not be happy with him just turning up, but he had to see her and find out what the hell was going on. Suddenly a black hackney with a yellow for hire sign showing appeared heading in the opposite direction. Rab forced it to stop for him by standing in the middle of the street. The driver looked concerned but finally agreed to take him.

Within five minutes it was pulling up outside Tracy's flat on Raploch Street. 'That will be nine pounds fifty.' The electronic speaker in the rear passenger cab said the words in a flat monotonous robotic tone. Rab searched his jeans for his wallet and then impatiently rifled through his jacket. It was not there; he could only surmise that he had dropped it during the altercation at the Caledonian. He reached for the door handle, only to find it was locked. The robot voice kicked in again but this time with a hint of resigned sarcasm. 'Cannie leave the taxi until you produce nine pounds fifty mate.' Rab edged his face up to the Perspex screen separating him from the driver.

'Av lost ma wallet, I'll need tae owe you it, pal.'

'Nae chance, you either pay up or I hit the alarm and the police will be called.'

The big man was no longer listening. He was watching in disbelief as another taxi pulled up outside the flat. It was Rab's double who jumped out and then ran around to the other side before opening the door and smiling. Tracy stepped out looking both glamorous and gorgeous. The other Rab was even wearing the same clothes that he had on. The happy couple walked arm in arm up to the close and disappeared inside.

'Open this fucking door ya bastard or I'll break the fucking thing down.' Rab had completely lost it now. He had to catch up with Tracy and find out who the imposter was. The taxi driver jumped out of the cab as Rab smashed his fists against the glass and screamed blue murder. The car indicators were flashing, and a panic alarm was screaming into the night. Within five minutes multiple blue lights had arrived to add to the scene of chaos.

The big man did not go down easy. It took five officers with pepper spray to finally get him in handcuffs and into the back of the van. Rab's eyes watered in pain with the sting of the spray as he rolled about kicking and screaming in the mobile cage. It was a pity that he did not get to see the police detective wearing an old suit who watched the commotion. If he had he might have been able to take in the look of satisfaction on the man's face. *I knew I would get you in the end mister big shot. It was just a matter of time. Cardboard gangsters like you always walk straight into the net. Easy.*

* * *

Rab placed the key into the door of his flat. His hands were shaking from both fear and lack of alcohol. He felt exhausted and dirty. The police had held him overnight and well into the next day. They had charged him with breach of the peace as well as resisting arrest and assaulting a police officer. The Big Man knew that he could be in real trouble. It was not unlikely that he might even get a short prison stretch as this was not the first time he had gone head-on with the fuzz. Once again though he had gotten away with a serious assault as the police had not been able to convince Joe Slash to press charges when they visited him in the hospital. Rab made a mental note to apologise to his mate once he got things sorted out. The Big Man had become so confused by drinking that he no longer knew what was real and what he had imagined. The one thing he was sure off was that he had to get his phone charged and call Tracy.

He walked into the living room looking for his charger and was stunned to see three full vodka bottles sitting on the table. *What the fuck, I don't remember buying them. What the hell is happening to me?' Well, one thing is for sure, I'm touching fuck all drink. That's me aff it for good. I need to get me, and Tracy sorted out.*

Rab for once stuck to his promise, well for now that is. He stripped off his dirty clothes and stood under the hot shower letting the steaming water try and wash away his troubles. It was now four in the afternoon. Tracy would finish her shift at six and he would call her before going round to her place with a bunch of flowers. The Big Man dried himself off and pulled his dressing gown around him before walking into the kitchen. Despite days of hardly eating anything he still did not feel hungry. Rab opened the cupboard and pulled out a tin of steak and kidney pie. He impatiently grabbed the tin opener and removed the lid before placing it in the oven on a medium heat. He walked back into his living room feeling like a cornered man. The three bottles of vodka stared at him as he sat in his favourite chair. They reminded him of the three wise monkeys, see no evil, speak no evil, and hear no evil. *I mean what harm could one wee drink do. Maybe just a couple while the phone charges up.*

As he opened the first bottle and poured himself a small one Rab heard the sound of mail dropping through his letterbox. He walked into the hallway before bending down to lift the four white envelopes from the floor. With an air of impatience, the Big Man ripped open one of them and a greetings card fell out. He read the words with a growing sense of dread and bewilderment.

Congratulations to both you and Tracy on your engagement. From your long-suffering mates at The Clachan. Soapy, Stevie Boy, Wee Tony, Paul, Joe Slash, Kendy, Lorna, She Wolf, and Jet Doll. Go for it, Big Rab.

The Big Man dropped the card onto the floor without opening the others. He walked back into the living room and took the open vodka bottle into his hands before placing it on his lips. Within seconds he had demolished half the contents and then poured the rest into a pint glass. Rab sat back down in his chair and waited for oblivion to take over and let him forget the world outside and all his troubles.

***

Rab could feel the shivers running through his aching body. His eyes were still closed, and his head was spinning. He dreaded opening them and having to face up to reality. *How long had he been out of it this time? Hours or days?* A picture of Tracy flashed across his brain as he remembered the engagement cards. *Maybe it had all been a dream. Yes, that's it, it all made sense now. He had been on a long bender that had stretched for days. The fights, Tracy, the engagement, his double walking into the flat, all of it had been made up by his drink-addled brain. It was time to wake up, stop the endless boozing, clear his head, and go and get his life sorted out.*

Rab tried desperately to open his eyes but it was not easy. His eyelids felt as though they were stuck together. He attempted to force his body to sit up, but it was impossible. Finally, he managed to rub the stickiness away from his eyelids and look around. Everything was blurred but he could make out the wardrobe in front of him and realised he was laying on his bedroom floor. He moved his head to the right and saw the side of the bed less than a foot away. His hands ran slowly down the side of his body as he felt his clothes. Even that tiny effort made him feel nauseous and exhausted. *Jesus, what a state to get into. I didn't even make it onto the bed, never mind take my clothes off.* He could smell the stench of stale vodka as his fingers touched a bottle standing beside him on the floor.

It was while he chastised himself with his thoughts that the strangeness of the situation started to dawn on him. His vision was still blurred, and his body could not move but he could hear the muffled sound of voices and excited exertion. The bedroom lamp was on giving a low light that was casting shadows on the wall to his right. He moved his head slowly to watch. The dancing figures at first confused him but then with growing horror, it began to dawn on Rab who it was and what they were doing. The shapes on the wall moved in unison with the grunts and panting of the couple as they reached a climax. The bed shook so violently that the leg close to Rab's head was bouncing off the wooden floor. 'Oh God Rab, oh Rab, Rab……….'

The Big Man lay on the floor still unable to move while tears ran down the sides of his face and onto the ground. He couldn't speak, only his head and arms could move but even that required a massive effort. He wanted to shout, scream, punch, kick, lash out at anything and everything, but it was impossible. All he could do was lay there and listen to the two lovers on the bed above him.

'Oh Rab, I really do love you. I thought we were finished the way you were going but you've changed. I'm so grateful.' She ran her hand down the side of his face and then kissed him.

'For you doll, anything. Maybe I just needed to grow

up. See things for what they really are. I promise you, me and the booze are over.' She kissed him again.

'I know, I believe you. Just take each day as it comes. But that's a while now, My God, even the gang in The Clachan are singing your praises.'

'Yes, well I'll probably stay away from the boozer completely from now on. I don't want to get into a situation where temptation might be in front of me. I promise you I'll not touch a drop until the day we finally get married.' He leaned forward on the pillow and kissed her forehead. 'I could murder a cup of coffee, Trace.' She smiled and within seconds was climbing out of the bed on the opposite side.

The Big Man watched her perfect naked body glide passed him as he lay on the floor. He tried desperately to shout Tracy, *it's me, the real Rab is here*, but all that came out was a faint guttural murmur. Her long legs and peach-shaped bottom disappeared through the bedroom door. He wanted to kill the imposter who had stolen his girl, but it was impossible. And then he heard the sound of movement and the rustling of bed covers. A face appeared from the side of the bed above him. His face, but a healthier one. A face that could talk with a body that could move. The man looked at him and Rab could make out a smile on his lips.

'You look terrible Big Man. You know what you need?' The Big Man again tried to reply but nothing came out. 'I think you need a hair of the dog. That will get you sorted out

Big Fella.' The imposter then jumped out of the bed stark naked. He violently lifted Rab's Head and took the three-quarter full vodka bottle in his other hand. 'Fancy a wee drink, Big Man? You know you can't resist it, have one on me. In fact, have the whole fucking bottle.'

In his mind, Rab was fighting, punching the man, desperately trying to resist what he was going to do. The reality was he was powerless. The imposter roughly forced the bottle between Rab's lips and emptied the contents into his mouth. The vodka ran down his throat choking him and then down the side of his face and onto the floor.

'Still just the one sugar for you Rab?' The last thing the Big Man heard was Tracy's voice shouting from the kitchen.

***

Rab woke up on the bedroom floor. He looked at his surroundings and could see that he was still fully clothed. Two empty vodka bottles lay beside him. At first, he felt a sense of relief at the realisation that he had been dreaming. How much of all this confusion was real and how much was drink-induced hallucination he was still not sure. Something was wrong though, he could sense it, but his brain was still befuddled by the alcohol. He sat up and wondered why everything looked so blurred and hazy. There was a strange smell, not just of stale vodka but something stronger. It was a burning smell.

Suddenly the realisation hit him like a ten-ton truck. The haze was smoke, and the smell was burning. *Oh Fuck, the steak pie.* Rab tried to stand up but he moved too quickly for a man still under the influence and instead he crashed forward towards the bedside table. His legs went from under him and his face slammed into the hard surface with a sickening thud.

Tracy walked out of the hospital having just ended a long night shift. She was tired, exhausted even but somehow, she felt good. She had a spring in her step. For the first time in years, she knew that her life was changing. Yes, she still had feelings for Rab, but they had gradually changed over the years to sympathy more than anything else. Tracy knew that she was moving on and her destiny would no longer have him and his drink problem standing in the way. She jumped into her car and started the engine. The wheels turned just a few revolutions and moved Tracy into the next stage of her life. One that was at long last not clouded by addiction and selfishness.

Another ambulance sped into the Accident and Emergency Bay of the hospital just as she was about to drive off. *Oh well, someone else can look after this one, I've done more than my fair share tonight.* Unfortunately, her colleagues would not have to do much. The Paramedics had tried their best, but the victim was too far gone. It was probably the smoke that killed Big Rab rather than the alcohol. But hey, it would have got him in the end anyway. At least he went out like a Viking as he was dragged from the burning building. The Big Man had always been destined to go out in a blaze of glory. Unfortunately, the reality was more death by steak pie and vodka.

Evolution

Can of lager, take a drink
Bacardi, brandy, vodka, whiskey, the kitchen sink
What's up with you, life is for living
Don't be a bore, let's party to an early death
Who's for a shot? Drink it straight
Your round, my round, who's round?
Pub, house guests, drinking alone
Spirits, beer, wine, meths, let's drink to an early death.
Once funny stories repeated endlessly
Reminiscences of the drinking bores
Weddings, funerals, engagements, holidays
Another reason to sink them quick
And once on your deathbed your only regret
You may miss the session they planned for you yet.

AVAILABLE FROM AMAZON OR RMPEARSON.NET

Selected Amazon Reviews

This is a book that managed to affect me deeply. Acutely thoughtful and at times really creepy, *The Path* is a ghost story that is at once desperately sad but also ultimately uplifting, and, in its own way, also cosy and comforting. I read loads of ghost stories every year- this is one of my favourites. (The Path)

***

Loved this book. I've read a few books from this author and I thought it would be hard to beat *Deadwater,* but this book has been by far the best. It was comical, enlightening, thoughtful, and scary. You get really involved with the characters. Would highly recommend (Scotland Shall Burn)

***

What an anthology. One of the best of the year for me. A style of book I haven't seen before as the author includes a written musing on the seasons of the year, between every two to three tales. This works so well it's almost worth the price of the book for these alone. There are no weak stories here, but three, in particular, stand out, what a clever baby will make you look at all infants in a brand-new light, our lady of the Quarry is a belter of a ghost story with a stunning twist. Harmonica seeks partner tells the heart-breaking tale of a lonely man and a homeless woman and how we all judge without knowing the whole story. All in all, 5 stars are not enough for this collection of tales. Would like to see more from this author. Here's hoping. (A Season for Ghosts)

***

The author details a thrilling story of the downfall of a successful Scottish businessman who chases his past to stop the destruction of his seemingly perfect life. Brilliantly written, with characters I really connected to. I couldn't put it down! (Broken Leaves)

***

One of the best books I've read in a long time. The characters were interesting, and I really felt a personal affiliation with the main ones. Rooting them to do well or in a few cases...rooting for their demise. It's great when you get so involved in a story that you stay up late reading it. There were some surprises, sad and happy moments. The era was well captured, bringing back memories of local police stations, village life and there was always a haunted house growing up. Loved this. Can't wait to read the next one (Deadwater)

* * *

First of all, it's obvious the author loves Scotland, I'm sure a number of the places mentioned in the book exist and chances are he knows them all. Now on to the story, I just couldn't put it down, as a keen, now retired cyclist I lived every bump in the road the main character hit as he went touring for a week to get some respite from his ill wife who he left with a carer. Meeting a woman cyclist who herself hides a dark secret, the tale starts to take a darker route. Along the way he seems to see something following them and no matter how far they travel the spectre always pursues. This is a fantastic tale about how a person can be haunted in a way that few supernatural stories have touched on before. The ending I assure you, you will never see coming, and if I could give 6 stars I would. Highly recommended. (Porcelain)

* * *

Read until the wee hours of the morning and finished

it after breakfast. Although a poignant, often sad story, I did find myself smiling throughout when the author's humour flashed from Grant to light up the pages. Both Grant and Maggie were portrayed sympathetically and with real insight. Eve's story was heart-breaking and the porcelain lady finally, eventually, tragically, made sense. The ending wasn't signposted. I really didn't see it coming. I had a whole other explanation worked out in my head, so it was a real surprise when it came. The best ghost stories are subtle. The best of the best incorporate a narrative that affects the reader at some deep level. This story delivered. (Porcelain)

The Path by Richard M Pearson

On a path filled with ghosts and secrets, nobody is safe.

For neurotic Ralph and easy-going Harvey, the trek across the remote, rolling hills of Scotland is a chance to get away from life, an opportunity to rediscover their place in the world. At least that's the plan. But they are two middle-aged, unfit men trying to cross one hundred miles of rugged terrain.

Despite that, they might have had a chance if that was their only problem. Unfortunately, not only are they alcoholics, someone or something is stalking them, watching their every move. Worse, one man carries a terrible secret about why he went on the trip. A secret that will turn a friendly trek into something far darker. It's a safe bet that if either man survives, he will never be the same again.

The Path is the first novel by Richard M Pearson. A gothic ghost story for modern times that builds up an atmosphere of foreboding and fear.

(Amazon review)

A terrific read. I thoroughly enjoyed this novel. Atmospheric, melancholic, laced with pathos and wry humour. Excellent plot and an intriguing outcome. Strong characterisation, complex and endearing personas, more so for their flaws and imperfections. The poems were also a nice touch. Almost offering a staging post for the author's state of mind as each chapter ends. I can highly recommend The Path, it won't disappoint.

(Available from Amazon)

Website, Rmpearson.net

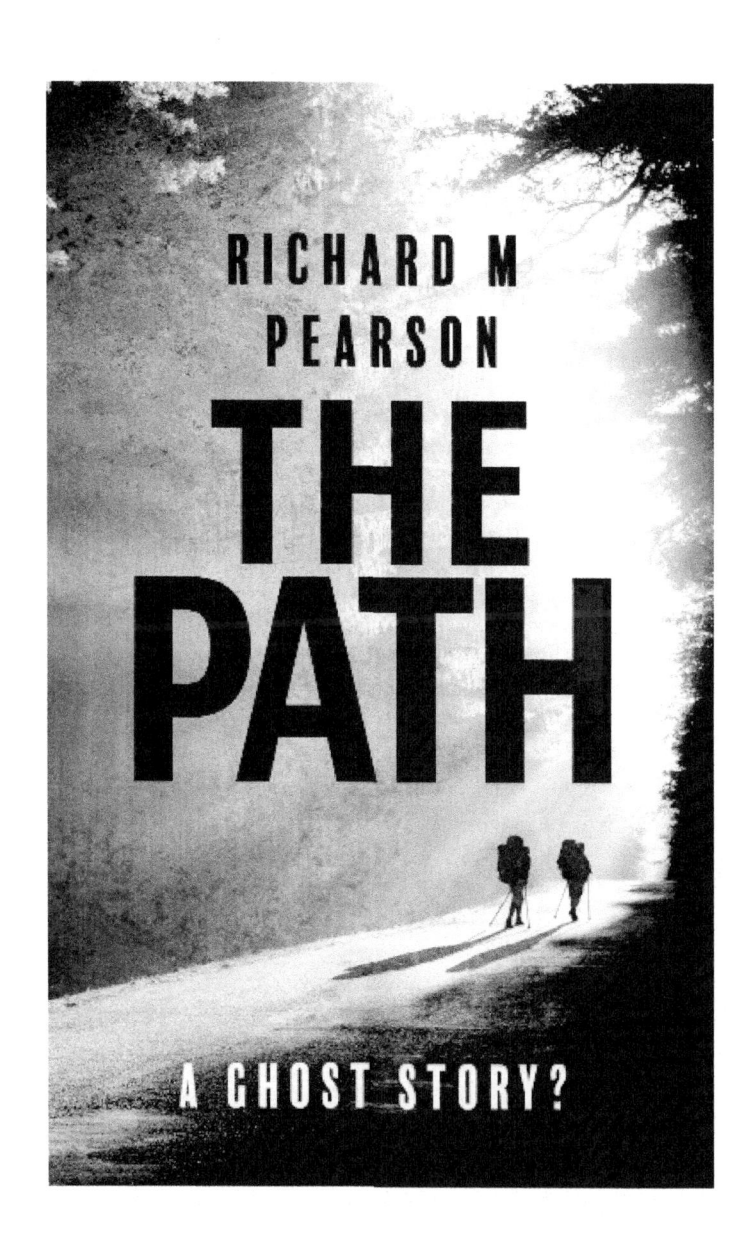

RICHARD M PEARSON

THE PATH

A GHOST STORY?

Deadwater by Richard M Pearson

Who would dare to unlock the secret of Deadwater Mansion?

It is only when you look back at things from the distance of many years that you finally understand why. The problem was we in the village blamed the aristocratic Denham-Granger family for our bad fortune. Everything was their fault according to us but in hindsight, that was more to do with jealousy than reality. We hated them because they had wealth and looked down on us as uneducated peasants.

But the truth was, they were as much victims as we were. No, the real holder of all the power through the years was Deadwater. The grand three-story country mansion cast its shadow over the village and manipulated everything to survive. So, when it realised that time was running out it played the final card, and then dark retribution crawled out of that room to hunt each of its victims down.

Deadwater, A Classic Gothic Ghost Story with a shocking twist.

(Available from Amazon)

Website, Rmpearson.net

FROM THE AUTHOR OF 'THE PATH'

RICHARD M PEARSON
DEADWATER
WHO CAN FREE THE SECRET OF DEADWATER HOUSE?

Broken Leaves by Richard M Pearson

Only she knows the terrible secret of his past.

A dark thriller to keep you reading through the night.

One moment of madness in his youth has caught up with Matt Cunningham. The only person who can save the successful business executive is his alcoholic ex-lover Roni Paterson. But how do you find a woman who has disappeared for thirty years and what if she becomes part of the unfolding nightmare?

Blackmail, Murder, Love, Hate. There is nowhere left to hide when revenge comes calling.

(Amazon review)

I cannot recommend this book highly enough. Thoroughly enjoyed it and could not put it down from the minute I started it. The plot kept me guessing until the end and the characterisations were fantastic. Such a believable story and so well written. Five stars. This is the third book I have read by this author so if you're looking for an excellent read, I would recommend this along with The Path and Deadwater.

(Available from Amazon)

Website, Rmpearson.net

From the author of
'The Path' and 'Deadwater'

BROKEN LEAVES

THERE IS NOWHERE LEFT TO HIDE

WHEN REVENGE COMES CALLING

RICHARD M PEARSON

A SEASON FOR GHOSTS
FOUR SEASONS, NINE DARK TALES

Step into the Shadow.

It is time to meet the talking baby, become trapped alone in the snow at an isolated railway station, meet the weirdest flight cabin crew ever, go on blind dates with ghostly women and walk 800 miles through the frozen wastes to find the crumbling castle of Blackbarron. And then, only then will the tall man come looking for you.

Nine stories to keep you awake at night. Nine dark tales to haunt your dreams.

(Available from Amazon)

Website, Rmpearson.net

From the author of 'The Path' and 'Deadwater'

A SEASON FOR GHOSTS

Four Seasons, Nine Dark Tales.
Step into the Shadow.

RICHARD M PEARSON

PORCELAIN

WILL SHE NEVER SET HIM FREE?

That day I set out on my bike for a week of cycling around the borders I did not believe in ghosts. Maybe if I am being honest, I did not even believe in people anymore. For six days I charged headlong into relationships, friendships, and trouble. It was not just what was in front of me that made the journey so memorable. No matter who I met or where I ended up, she was always following in my shadow. At the time I had no idea who she was or what I had done to deserve the porcelain lady hunting me down. I know now of course, but it is too late to save me. Guilt or reality? As the week went on, I lost the ability to know the difference. The one thing I always understood from the start was that the journey had to end with just the two of us confronting each other at long last.

He had seven days left, she had forever.

(Available from Amazon)

Website, Rmpearson.net

From the author of *The Path* and *Deadwater*

PORCELAIN

Will she never set him free?

RICHARD M PEARSON

Printed in Great Britain
by Amazon